Lots of love,

Savi

EVERYONE HAS A STORY – 2

SAVI SHARMA

First published by Westland Publications Private Limited in 2018

61, 2nd Floor, Silverline Building, Alapakkam Main Road, Maduravoyal, Chennai 600095

Westland and the Westland logo are the trademarks of Westland Publications Private Limited, or its affiliates.

ISBN: 9789387894129

10 9 8 7 6 5 4 3 2 1

This is a work of fiction. Names, characters, organisations, places, events and incidents are either products of the author's imagination or used fictitiously.

Typeset in Sabon Roman by SÜRYA, New Delhi
Printed at Thomson Press (India) Ltd.

Dedicated to:

YOU, ALWAYS

'The story of life can be summarised in a few short words. It is never-ending. No matter what you are going through, no matter how difficult the journey is, no matter how fate tests us, life never stops; it endures.'

PROLOGUE

Just because one turns to the final page, the final word of a book, it doesn't mean the story is complete. 'The End' is only a hopeful thought. Enjoy the satisfaction while you can, because change is inevitable.

There is no happily ever after. When that book closes, do you think that the characters just dance away to some sunny meadow with music and birdsong?

I am here to tell you that life is a constant test. People who haven't realised that are fools.

Those tests, those trials never end. I know that this is true; in fact, I can promise you that this is true.

How willing are you to persevere? Will you fight for that next bit of happiness, that next patch of sunlight after a gloomy day?

Or are you going to fail? Are you going to run away from the challenge, throwing your hands up in defeat?

One of the most powerful forces in the world is hope. Hope finds its way into the darkest rooms, sneaking its fingers around any blockades. No matter what is going on in your life, hope is a constant factor. Persistent and tenacious, it lifts people up and gives them a reason to dream.

If hope is suddenly removed, tossed away like a discarded tissue, there is little left. Without the cloak of hope, people buckle under the pressures that they face every day.

That is not necessarily a bad thing, in my opinion. What people don't get is that it is not your circumstances that control your life, but you.

Conflict is put on your path to determine how far you will go to succeed. Our lives are supposed be difficult, because if they were too easy, what would we learn? Nothing. People need to be tested to see how willing they are to fight.

And how soon you will give up.

Perhaps some people who pass those tests will receive tremendous rewards. Everybody gets knocked over by life, but a strong person gets up and walks once more.

But for those who do not pass the challenge, regret and sadness will dog them for a very, very long time. They will be surrounded by oppressive, shadowy doubts.

It's easy to make an excuse. It's harder to act to regain control of your life. Perhaps it doesn't matter, though. We may impact the people around us, but we are barely a drop of water in all the oceans.

The unknown is not a bad thing. Not seeing where your life is going to end up keeps you on your toes, looking to see what's around the next bend.

On the surface, it appears simplistic. But it's not.

These tests determine who will realise their dreams ... and who will be nagged by regret and doubt for the rest of their lives.

Will you stand and fight? Will you tackle your challenges aggressively? Will you lie and cheat? Or will you push through, rising to the challenge with optimism and determination?

Or will you give up?

Because life is not about being happy all the time. Things happen. People get sick; couples grow apart and break up. For those who think a happy ending is the end, think again. There is always another page, another chapter. That happy ending is only a happy pause in life.

There is always more to the story.

How do I know what I'm talking about? Who am I?

I am the darkest shades of black and the lightest shades of white.

I am life's trials.

I am fate.

And I am here to test your favourite characters, your beloved friends, the people who gave you hope and courage. The people who made you believe in your dreams. I am here to test Meera, Vivaan, Kabir, Nisha, and many others. I am here to destroy them, and I will. Just wait and watch.

Are you ready? Or are you scared?

1

MEERA

The slanting shadows in the room drew a stark finger across the coffee table, signalling the now sunny day outside. The morning had started off a bit dreary, with rain threatening to fall, but there never was any precipitation. Finally, the clouds surrendered, giving way to strong, afternoon sunshine.

Lifting my face to the late-day sun, I closed my eyes, living my memories behind shut eyelids. Drawing in a deep breath, I inhaled the warm satisfaction of a contented life. My shoulders lifted with the expanse of air in my lungs, and then lowered as I exhaled with a small purr.

Eyes still closed, I rolled my head slowly. It felt so good to stretch my muscles after sitting at my desk for so many hours.

Although my days are busy, writing in my journal seems to prompt other memories, not just the ones I'm writing down. Today, I savoured some of those memories, looking back at the last three years. They have been amazing years. Not only did I have Vivaan in my life, but I realised my dream of becoming a writer, with two successful books so far and a third being written.

Every day is a new source of excitement for me. Everyone has a story, it's true, and I loved the one that was being written about my life.

Slowly, I turned my face back towards my mahogany desk. Finally, I allowed my eyelids to lift, first peeking through my eyelashes and refocusing as they opened more.

A smile played on my lips as I reread the journal entry in front of me. I knew my lips were moving slightly as the words played through my mind. Vivaan teased me when I did this, but it was how I best saw the world on the pages in front of me.

I picked up my pen. Heavy, but beautifully balanced, the pen was a gift, a show of support for my career, and I loved feeling its weight as I wrote.

A soft knock sounded at the door.

'Yes?' I responded lazily.

'Meera?' a young woman's voice called through the heavy door. 'The man from the magazine is here for your interview.'

'Ah, yes,' I returned, smiling. I tucked my pen between the pages and closed my beloved diary. A glance at the clock confirmed that he was right on time. 'Can you please show him in?'

I stood, my bare toes sinking into the thick grey carpeting before I slipped my shoes back on. I glanced down quickly to make sure no stray crumbs from breakfast were clinging to my shirt. There were none. Casual, presentable. Perfect. I murmured a command to my music player and the volume turned down immediately. I loved that device.

The door swung open and a slightly heavyset man sauntered in, eyes dancing over the sharp lines in the room, the happy pictures on the walls. I waited patiently. When he finished his appraisal, with a grin, I reached out my hand to shake his.

'Hi, I'm Meera,' I said warmly. 'Welcome to my home.'

He took my hand, pumping it firmly. I prided myself on having a firm handshake, but quickly adjusted my grip to apply an even more steady, firm grasp.

'Sai Patel,' he replied. 'Thank you for allowing me to interview you.'

'Of course,' I said. 'It's my pleasure.' I looked over the man's shoulder where my assistant, Aashi, was standing patiently. Although young, in her early twenties, Aashi was determined to prove her worth despite the fact that she was inexperienced and a recent college dropout. In my mind, I knew that, with a little patient guidance, the young woman's interests in her education would be rekindled.

Aashi cocked her head slightly, hands clasped in front of her. 'Would you like me to bring in some refreshments?'

I turn a questioning look at Sai, who nodded eagerly. 'I am a little ... thirsty,' he said somewhat sheepishly.

'Aashi,' I said, 'would you mind bringing in two cappuccinos?' I couldn't help but tease, drawing out the idea of more refreshments a little before I continued. 'And perhaps some of the butter cookies I baked yesterday?'

Sai cleared his throat happily. 'You bake too?' he asked, plopping down into the soft brown leather chair in front of my desk.

I nodded and settled myself back into the black desk chair. 'I don't get much time in the kitchen, I'm afraid,' I admitted. It was true. I'll never be the culinary artists that my friend Kabir and his wife Nisha are, but I do love to bake. 'Though when I do, I find it clears my head and breaks up the monotony of a long day at the desk. This is one of my grandmother's recipes, so I hope you'll enjoy the biscuits.'

'I'm sure I will.' Seemingly contented knowing that food was on its way, Sai began to rustle through his beaten-up satchel before bringing out a small recorder.

'Do you mind?' he asked. Of course, I shook my head, agreeing to his request. Recording my words protects me as much as it protects him. This way, I can't be misquoted. 'First,' he said, almost as an afterthought, 'I must congratulate you on the success of your first two books.'

'Have you read them, then?'

He blushed and nodded happily. 'Most definitely. It's why I begged my editor for this assignment. I really wanted to meet the woman behind this great success. You'd have to live under a rock not to have heard of both your books.'

I smiled. 'That is kind,' I said. It always made me feel humble when I heard praise like this. 'I'm glad that it has been an inspiration for some. And I hope the third book will offer as much encouragement as my previous two books.'

Sai nodded and turned his attention back to the recorder, fumbling with the switch. Finally, he placed it on the glass table in front of him. Then, he fished around in his satchel and pulled out a small notebook and pen.

I must have shifted in my seat because his eyes snapped back to full attention on me. 'How are you after the accident?'

'I am much, much better. Really, completely healed. Thank you for asking.'

Flipping his notebook open to a fresh page, he absently rolled his pen between his fingers before continuing. 'So, tell me. You truly brought your characters to life in the first book, perhaps because they are based on real people?'

I nodded. 'I believe that this is part of the magic, yes. But it's not necessarily the people themselves—although, of course, they are my friends. I think it was their journeys that made the book so special. And the journeys were the inspiration.'

'Tell me more about the inspiration,' he pressed.

I closed my eyes and took a deep breath. 'Sometimes,' I began, 'we move through life, seemingly unaware of what is going on around us. We go to work, we come home, we make a meal. We're living, but we're not really absorbing life.

'While these things are important, they are only one layer. Sort of like a sketch before it becomes a beautiful painting. Living life to the fullest is about painting in the yellows of the laughter, the blues of the bird songs we hear, the reds of the sadness that pulls us down at times. And the purples as we spring back up, pushing past the darkness and striding with a purpose toward the good times.'

'And your book certainly does show this,' he said. 'What is writing a book like? For you?'

I smiled. 'Writing a book is … going on an amazing journey. You might have some idea of where you are heading, but you have no idea how the landmarks and events on the way will impact you.'

'Is it daunting to decide to write an entire book?'

'No,' I said. 'The words, like a sand castle, start to build around me until they create a great fortress from the tiniest letters.'

As he spoke, Aashi nudged her way past the half-closed office door with a tray of beverages and cookies. Sai's fingers danced eagerly in the air as she placed the tray on the table between us, then happily snatched a biscuit as soon as she stepped back.

Aashi quietly placed my cappuccino in front of me, met my eye and raised an elegantly arched eyebrow in a silent question. 'I think we are all set, for now, Aashi,' I responded to her non-question. 'Thank you so much.'

'Of course,' Aashi said, then glided across the room and closed the door behind her softly.

'So,' Sai continued. 'Tell me about how people have reacted to your books.'

I stood up and walked around my desk and piled three cookies in the palm of my left hand. If I didn't pounce on them now, I was afraid I wouldn't get the chance. Leaning casually against my desk, I responded.

'It has been amazing. Of course, when I started to write, it was with the hope that people would be open to my stories. I remember walking down a street one time, and there were a group of school kids, maybe in their mid-teens, I'm guessing. They were all bunched together, talking and having fun. I wouldn't have paid much attention, but as I walked by, I happened to glance at one of the kids. When he thought nobody was paying attention to him, he let that mask of the 'cool kid' fade away. I saw something on his face—pain, sadness, I don't know for sure. It was only there for a moment and then the smile came back, and he went back to laughing with his friends.

'I thought to myself, "There is a story in each and every one of us." It's not the façade that we put on when we are around our friends, our co-workers, or our family. It's what is in our hearts. It's our hopes, our dreams, our fears ...'

Sai munched thoughtfully on a cookie and nodded. 'I can see what you're saying, Meera. There are times when I interview people for an hour and walk out knowing that there is more to learn about them.'

'Exactly. And I think that these stories are important for us all to learn.'

'Why?'

'Because as much as we think we are individuals, we are influenced by so many different forces. We are not only formed by our experiences, but also by the people that have helped guide us, and sometimes, challenge us. Push us to be more than we are.'

As I spoke, I could feel an urgent energy rising up in me, effervescing.

'My books, my success so far, I believe is because I have been able to lasso these emotions and put words to them in a way that people can relate to the characters. They can see the people in my books, just as clearly as I can see you looking at the pile of cookies on the plate.'

Sai tore his eyes from the plate of food and looked at me once again, breaking into a grin. 'You caught me,' he laughed.

I joined in his laughter. 'I am glad you are enjoying them.'

'Oh, I am,' he said, patting his belly before going back to our conversation. 'You certainly have caught those emotions, much to the delight of your readers. Your books have certainly become an inspiration to many people.'

I said sincerely, 'I certainly hope so. My intent has always been to give my readers something to think about as they are navigating through their own lives. I want to inspire, to evoke a sense of drive in people. We all have the opportunity to improve our lives, every single day. We shouldn't sit idle and let life happen. We need to make it happen!'

I watched a little shiver ripple through Sai and I knew that he was not just hearing my words, but actually feeling them. He sat silently for a moment, as though he was thinking intently about something. Then, with a little shake, he smiled at me and returned to the interview. 'What can you tell me about this new book, then?'

'Not much, I'm afraid. I still need to finalise things with my publishers before we release too many details.'

'Just a hint?' he asked, leaning forward.

I knew he would ask, just as I knew it would be okay to give him a little taste of what was to come. 'It's about a starmaker,' I said.

I couldn't help it; I wanted to see the approval on his face. I still needed to know that this was a good idea. My publishers had liked the storyline, but they had a different agenda from my reader. My readers wanted to be inspired.

At the blank look on Sai's face, I knew I needed to give more information.

'Not like some fantasy,' I explained. 'This starmaker helps people achieve their dreams and become successful.'

I explained a little more, then trailed off as I watched him scribbling intently in his notebook. I gazed out of the window at the sky, relishing the warmth of the sun. I knew, the clouds would skate in from beyond the horizon soon.

He cleared his throat. 'Is the publishing deal finalised?'

I shook my head. 'I'll be meeting my publishers next week at the Delhi Lit Fest. We'll finalise things then.'

Sai popped yet another butter cookie in his mouth and crunched thoughtfully. 'That is why you're going there then?'

'Oh no,' I responded. 'That is part of it, of course, but not even the most important part. I am anxious to meet my peers, the other authors that will be there.'

'What do you hope for?' he asked.

My watch gave out a small chime, reminding me of the time. I glanced at it, subtly indicating the end of the interview. 'The world is wide open,' I responded to his question, shrugging my shoulders. 'I would no more dare guess what I will meet than I could tell you what I will be eating for breakfast a year from now. But I will tell you something: I am very, very excited to see what the future holds for me.'

Sai packed away his interviewing material, then stood and offered me his hand. I shook it warmly; then wrapped the remaining few biscuits in a napkin and silently offered them to him.

'Thank you,' he said, taking them happily and holding them like they were a cherished treat. 'They are most delicious.'

'You're welcome. And thank you for coming over today.' I reached behind my desk and retrieved my business card. 'Please, feel free to let me know if you need a clarification on anything or if you have any follow-up questions.'

Sai's eyes met mine. I knew from what he had said that he had wanted to meet me, but now I could see in his eyes that there was new admiration, not just curiosity about who I was. He slipped his own card out of his pocket. 'And for you,' he said, handing the dog-eared information over to me. 'If there is anything to add, please let me know. Travel safely to Delhi, and best of luck to you, Meera.'

I walked him to the door and we said our goodbyes once more. I watched him drive away from my little house and leaned against the door, going over our conversation in my head. I loved being able to speak about my experiences. I always hoped that these interviews helped inspire people as much as my writing. Maybe Sai would go home and start writing his own book.

As I returned to my office with the intention of clearing up after our snack, my phone rang.

I picked it up, but had no time to get my hello out. 'What time will you be here?' the man on the phone said without preamble.

'And hello to you,' I laughed at my friend, Kabir. 'I'll be there in about half an hour.'

'Great,' Kabir said enthusiastically. 'Looking forward to it.'

'Me too,' I agreed. 'It's going to be a night to remember, for sure.'

Pressing the button to end the call, my eyes danced over to the picture of Vivaan on the wall. 'I'll see you soon,' I said softly, blowing the photograph a gentle kiss. I knew he'd be picking me up any minute now, so I grabbed the brightly wrapped gift that was lying on the table, stroking my fingers over the pink and white bow.

Wandering into the kitchen, I let Aashi know that Sai had left and that I would be leaving soon as well. We quickly went over the schedule for the next day, and then I went back into my office to call Vivaan.

2

VIVAAN

Squinting in the bright sun, my fingers found their way to the compartment above the windshield. I tapped it once and it opened, giving me the sunglasses I suddenly needed. The day was partly cloudy when I started driving, but the brilliant sun presented itself as I navigated through the traffic to get to Meera's house.

My phone rang, that special tone that I had programmed in to let me know, without even looking, that Meera was calling me. I really didn't need the ringtone; most of the time, I reached for my phone to answer it before she even called. We had such a powerful connection.

I slipped my sunglasses on and put the phone on speaker. 'Hello, sunshine,' I said happily.

'Sunshine now?' Meera laughed. 'Or are you talking to the sky?

I felt the laughter well up from deep inside me. 'It seemed fitting in this late afternoon weather. But yes, I was speaking to you. Can you hear me okay? I'm driving right now, so I have you on speaker phone.'

'I can hear you just fine,' Meera responded. 'Glad you're remembering to put it on speaker. Don't want to tempt fate or anything.'

'No way,' I answered firmly.

'How has your day been going?' she asked. I loved that no matter what was going on in her own day, she always took the time to ask me about my day. It warmed me to know how much she cared about me.

I responded that my day had gone very well, and then remembered that she had an interview today. 'Did your interview go well?' I asked. 'Did he or she like the cookies you made? I still can't believe you wouldn't let me eat any,' I grumbled teasingly.

'The interview went very well and he loved the cookies. I do have a confession to make though.'

'Oh?' I asked. I could tell by the way she was talking that it wasn't too serious, though.

She cleared her throat. 'I... um... gave him the rest of the cookies.'

I rolled my eyes. She was always giving away food. She'd bake two loaves of bread, only to give one to a neighbour or something. 'I'd be crushed but that doesn't surprise me,' I admitted. 'Plus, I know you'll make me more.'

'Oh, you think so, do you? Maybe I wasn't planning on it.'

'You weren't going to make me more cookies?' I asked in mock horror.

'Of course I am.'

'I knew it!'

Meera laughed. I loved that laugh. 'You know me too well,' she said.

'Never too well,' I responded. 'Just the perfect degree of "Knowing Meera".'

'Knowing Meera,' she said. 'When I'm old and grumpy, maybe that is what I'll name my memoirs. Anyway... what time do you think you'll be here?'

I glanced over at the landmarks around me. It amazed me how quickly I was absorbed in my conversation. It was almost as if I were in the same room as my girlfriend, instead of weaving through the busy Pune traffic. 'I should be there in about ten minutes,' I confirmed. 'Will you be ready by then?'

'Always ready for you,' she said.

We said our goodbyes and I pressed the button to disconnect the call.

I must be the luckiest man alive, I mused. *I have a fantastic woman in Meera, who is everything to me. I still thank the heavens that I crossed paths with her four years ago. Imagine, if I was ten minutes late to the café, or she was sick the day I was there... fate would never have brought us together.*

In the silence of the car, I laughed at myself. *Fate would have found a way, regardless. She and I were meant to be together, always.*

From the first moment, she possessed my thoughts. I wanted to tell her what was in my heart, but my emotions and my words never connected. Eventually, they did and look at us now.

Thinking of the day that I met Meera reminded me of how fortunate I was also to have had the chance to get to know Kabir. Happy, but driven to make his business succeed, his ambition and friendly nature made him very approachable. He and I became the best of friends, but he also extended himself to others. It was what made his business venture, Kafe Kabir, extremely successful.

I, in turn, was lucky to have invested in his business when he decided to start his own coffee shop. My investment yielded enough for me to be able to explore my own beloved country.

It was amazing, I thought, how much my desires were now tuned into India. When I met Meera, I was driven to escape the borders and travel the world. I wanted to see so many new things. I wanted to experience other foods, meet exotic people, dip my toes in waters I had only watched on TV. I loved looking at maps. Small maps, large maps, the globe. India seemed so small and there was so much to see.

How naive I was then, I thought to myself. I was hopping on to airplanes, sleeping in strange hotels, because I wanted to see ... what? The world? Yes, I travelled and, yes, I met some fascinating people.

But in doing so, I was missing so much. I overlooked the beauty of my own country.

Now, my drive to explore kept me so much closer to home. What changed? I think maybe it started the day Meera and I went to the old fort and my eyes opened to the beauty around me. I didn't need to cross the globe to see the beauty of the world. It was right here.

For the last three years, I had kept myself much closer to home. I now journeyed throughout India to find those small, less travelled areas. Those spots that do not come up at the top of a Google search, but are nestled away. This was the true beauty of India.

Meera and I had forged an amazing relationship. At first, we thought we could combine our work. She could travel with me, and write in hotels while I went off to learn more about our motherland.

It wasn't to be. If I were honest with myself, I think she was as drawn to her home office as I was drawn to the open road. I loved finding and then taking that path less travelled as much as she loved just being home. When we were finally honest with ourselves, and each other, we realised we needed to go in two different directions.

One might think that this would mean our relationship was doomed to fall apart, but that couldn't be further from the truth. Our relationship grew even stronger.

Now, I traveled about three weeks of the month, while she stayed home in Pune. Then, the fourth week or so, I joined her in our city.

Sometimes, she came with me; other times, her schedule didn't allow it. If she was on some self-imposed deadline, she wanted to just be in her familiar writing area. If she had commitments that I could attend, I went with her. At other times, she went alone.

It worked for us. Very well, in fact.

As my car moved closer to Meera's home, I thought about my next steps with work. I wanted to share what I had learned with other people... maybe those who had never taken the time to explore India, or maybe those who once thought, like I did, that they needed to leave our country's borders to really begin to live.

A few minutes from home, I decided once and for all that this is what I wanted to do. I wanted to start a company introducing other people to India. I needed to show my fellow countrymen just what we have within our own borders.

Just as I was pulling down Meera's street, my phone rang again. I pressed the button to receive the call. 'Look out your window and you'll see me,' I laughed.

I was barely out of the car when Meera came bursting out of her front door. She threw her arms around me and hugged me tightly. I returned the hug, savouring the scent of her hair as it fell over my face. We pulled away, and kissed the kiss of two people who had been apart much too long ... even though it had only been since yesterday.

'Hello to you too,' I said, laughing, when we stopped to catch our breath. 'Do you have the present?'

Meera held up one finger. 'Just inside the door,' she responded, and turned to prance back to the door. 'I had a feeling you would have smashed it when we said hello.'

I would have argued and tried to convince her that I would never have crushed something as precious as that gift. But I remembered our kiss and knew it would have been a useless argument.

3

KABIR

My beautiful café was even more colourful than ever. Colours were splashed on the walls, spread over the tables, and floating in the air. Even if you weren't able to take in the colours, the sense of excitement in everyone was contagious and growing.

But something was missing. I took my phone out of my pocket yet again and frowned at the time. Opening my text message app, I tapped a quick question to my wife: 'Where are you?'

I got a response back almost immediately and wondered if she was starting her own message instead of simply responding to mine: 'I'll be there in about fifteen minutes.'

Nisha was the most reliable woman in the world. She was so steady, my rock. After a long day at work, I knew I could go home to a warm, delicious-smelling house and ease myself into her arms. I loved how she took care of me. Even after the baby came, her love just seemed to divide, pouring over me as well as our little girl.

A noise from the kitchen brought me back to the task at hand. The party. I hurried into the kitchen to check on the cake. 'Is it ready?' I asked my baker. She nodded and stepped back from the counter, her arms spread in invitation.

'Come, look,' she responded. 'It's a cake worthy of a queen... or a two-year-old princess.'

I looked it over with a critical eye, but it was absolutely perfect. I gave my baker a quick squeeze on the shoulder in gratitude. 'You're right; you did an amazing job.'

'As always,' she teased.

I nodded, laughing. 'As always.'

How was it that Jianna, our little baby, was two years old already? It seemed like just yesterday that Nisha told me she was pregnant. Although I had just started Kafe Kabir and we weren't in the best place financially, I was thrilled to know that Nisha was carrying my child. I loved watching my baby grow inside her, and it didn't seem like it could get any better. And then my sweet little girl was born, and life did get even more miraculous.

Soft murmuring broke into my reverie and I knew our guests were starting to arrive. I gave my baker a final nod of appreciation and headed back to the restaurant area to start greeting people.

I knew it would be a large turnout, probably larger than most birthday parties for a two-year-old. But Nisha and I agreed that it was important to invite not just our friends, but many of our regular customers as well. After all, they were an important part of our lives. They helped make Kafe Kabir a great success.

But even more than that, they were family. Perhaps not related by blood, but over the last few years, we have all shared joys, concerns, and celebrations. People came to the café when they were having a bad day, or just to share a bit of good news.

As the owner, one of my favourite things was to be able to gift a customer with a free pastry to share in their celebration—a new job, or a birthday.

I couldn't always go out into the world to see the play a customer was in, or visit someone I knew was sick in the hospital. But I could give away things, and that made me feel good.

I started to blow up a couple more balloons, and let my mind wander. The first time I ever gave anything away was so long ago. A sad young woman had walked into the café where I worked. She seemed so lost and lonely. I wanted to hug her, but I made her a drink with ice cream and pushed it across the counter to her... even before she could place an order.

That woman was Nisha, and my little gesture was the bit of kindness she needed on a very bad day.

So, without planning or discussing it, Nisha and I have both tried to help our customers when we could.

Even though a grateful smile or a thank you is all we would ever want, Nisha and I learned quickly that we genuinely touched many hearts, and people were eager to return the kindness. The minute Nisha's pregnancy was evident, customers were quick to ask after her when she wasn't in the café. Small gifts were brought—a rattle here, a knit baby sweater there—and oh, the flowers we were sent when our precious Jianna was born.

We were all in this together and I was delighted that so many people would be here to celebrate our little one's birthday.

My cell phone rang again, and I quickly excused myself and found a quiet area to take the call.

'I wanted to confirm our meeting tomorrow,' my realtor said on the phone. 'Do you have the address?'

I thought about the pile of paperwork that was sitting under the counter. 'Absolutely. It's at 3 pm, right?'

'Exactly,' she said. 'I'm glad you'll be able to make it. It sounds like you're really busy right now!'

I laughed. 'It's my daughter's birthday party. We're having it at the café. If you're in the area, you should stop by.'

'Wish I could, but I have too much to do today.'

'I understand. Goodbye for now.'

As I walked back into the café, Nisha was rushing in the door at the same time as Meera and Vivaan did. Even though Nisha was a little later than she anticipated, I loved seeing the three of them coming in together.

Even though Meera and Vivaan were both extremely busy people too, when the four of us were able to gather together, it was almost like coming home from a long journey.

Jianna held out her long arms to me, and I swept her up, giving Nisha a tight hug as well before we kicked the party into high gear.

The life of the party, Jianna, seemed to coax a smile out of everybody she turned her beautiful brown eyes on. And although we said gifts were not necessary, our little girl had plenty of unwrapping to do, and she took to the task with delighted wonder. In fact, I was just as amazed at how generous people were to our little girl.

'Thank you so much, everyone,' I said, looking around the room at all these familiar faces. We were truly fortunate, I thought, as I reached over and squeezed Nisha's hand.

'Thank us with some cake,' Vivaan suggested loudly, right before Meera gave him a playful shove, rolling her eyes dramatically.

Before we cut the cake, though, I had something important I wanted to say.

Clambering on a chair, I asked for everyone's attention. 'Thank you for coming today,' I began with a huge smile, looking at all the happy faces in the café. 'You have all been a very important part of our lives, and Nisha and I are very grateful for your support of our little family.' I looked down at my beautiful wife's face and she nodded her agreement, eyes shimmering with happy tears.

'We are all here to celebrate Jianna's birth. It's been a fun two years... a few sleepless nights but ones that I wouldn't trade for the world. Jianna has blossomed with so much love in her world and everyone here is partially responsible for that.'

My eyes glided over the people gathered and I gave them a huge grin. 'I look forward to celebrating many more of Jianna's birthdays with you.'

I looked over at our precious girl who was wriggling in Nisha's arms. What an amazing miracle that little one was. I felt my heart swell as I thought about how full my life felt with my little family.

'I also want to thank three very important people in my life.' I nodded at Meera. 'Thank you, Meera, for believing in me when I didn't even believe in my own abilities. Your encouragement was very, very important to me when you encouraged me to follow my own dreams to start the café.' Meera's lips were pressed together in a smile.

'Vivaan,' I continued, 'your financial investment in Kafe Kabir was instrumental, but even more than that, your trust in me and my dream is more valuable than any price tag. Thank you, my dear friend.' Meera and Nisha both gave him a little hug and Meera pecked a happy kiss on his cheek.

'And Nisha,' I said, holding my clasped hands over my heart. Unconsciously, my wife made the same gesture. 'I can't thank you enough for your constant support, not only as my wife but as my best friend as well. I would be a hell of a man without you to give me meaning.'

Although only a few steps away, my sweet wife blew me a kiss as I continued my speech. For a moment, I watched as Jianna successfully slid off her mother's hip and held fast to Nisha's fingers, so she could toddle around. The baby's face broke into a huge, drool-filled grin.

'I am beyond excited at how well Kafe Kabir has grown over the last few years. Vivaan has been a tremendous asset in marketing our café. I know he mentions our café when he is away from home because we have many people who seek out Kafe Kabir when they are visiting from other regions.

'And of course, Meera's book and the stories she wove with such beautiful words, has helped make Kafe Kabir a very familiar name in many households. In short, she has made our café a destination for her readers. Thank you both, my friends,' I said nodding to the happy couple once more.

'I know you're all anxious to try that beautiful cake,' I laughed, 'but I have one more announcement. Very shortly, we will be opening a second location. Soon, you will be able to enjoy the same amazing coffee and delicious pastries in another section of Pune.'

'Where?' a voice yelled from the back.

I grinned. 'I'm looking at another place tomorrow but a final decision on the location hasn't been made yet. I have a few ideas, but there are quite a few other locations that I want to visit first.'

'Can you give us a hint?'

'Not until I know more,' I responded. 'But I am sure that, due to Vivaan's marketing talent, the location will be made public before the ink is even dry on the agreement.'

The audience clapped enthusiastically as I climbed down from my chair into a happy, enormous hug from Nisha, and then one from Meera. Vivaan shook my hand enthusiastically. Stepping back, I could see the pride in their eyes and I felt a sense of satisfaction bubbling up deep within me.

Walking behind the counter, I started cutting the cake to put on plates. I held the first one out for Nisha, who settled Jianna on her lap. Everyone watched and let out a collective 'awww' as my daughter grabbed a fistful of cake and jammed it into her mouth.

I wanted to watch her, but our guests were hungry too. Vivaan stood beside me and helped hand out the plates to people. I was so glad that we decided on such a large cake, as I handed out plate after plate of creamy sweetness.

After handing out a few second pieces and fielding a lot of questions about Jianna—everything from who took care of her when Nisha and I were at the café to jokes and predictions about her chosen career—the tidal wave of hungry people finally subsided. I handed Vivaan a plate and noticed the serious look on his face for the first time that evening.

I knew that look; I saw it in the mirror every time I thought about opening my own café, and then again when I first started thinking about opening the second location. Looking over my shoulder, I asked one of my staff to take over cutting the cake for those who wanted second pieces. She took a quick bite of her cake—yes, it was that good—and took over the cake-cutting duties.

'Can we talk?' Vivaan asked. 'Meera and Nisha grabbed a table in the corner.'

'Of course,' I responded, praying that nothing was wrong. I followed Vivaan through the busy café and sat down at the table, enjoying the relief in my legs as I settled into a chair. I reached over and took Jianna onto my lap so Nisha could clean the sticky icing off her hands. 'Is everything okay?'

'I was wondering the same thing,' Meera joined in, her eyes dancing over Vivaan's slightly tense figure.

In response, Vivaan nodded. 'I am fine, but I've made a decision about something,' he began, folding his hands together. 'Right now, it's just a thought but it's something I would like to move forward with. Before I go any further with it, I'd like to talk it over with the three of you.'

'Okay,' Meera said, her voice a mixture of hesitation and curiosity.

'You see, my friends,' he continued, looking at each of us slowly, 'just like you, there is something I would like to do. Something that I have been dreaming of doing.'

4

VIVAAN

I wasn't sure why I was so nervous telling them about my vision. Maybe it was because once it took shape in my mind, it came to life so ferociously that I was almost afraid my friends would reject the idea. Or they would come up with a reason why it wouldn't make sense.

I took a deep breath, and my mind returned to the moment I had the idea. I was at the Masrur Temples at the Reserve Jangal Masrur Joni-I. There was a light mist in the air as I walked through the ruins of the sandstone temples.

At first, I examined the intricate carvings, no doubt less defined than when they were originally created, and wondered what the other Siskara temples looked like before they were destroyed in a large earthquake in the early 1900s. Then, I sat on the other side of the rectangular reservoir in front of the temples, taking in their reflection in the greenish water.

I was in awe and was suddenly struck with an urge to share this with someone. Meera, of course; I loved it when she travelled with me. But others as well.

No pictures could do this amazing scene justice, just like many of the other beautiful places in my homeland. I was not a writer like Meera. I couldn't put together the right words to tell people about the Masrur Temples or any of the other wonders I had seen.

Suddenly, I felt a purpose, as strong and hardened as the ruins in front of me. That purpose was to bring people here, to show them the beauty of India.

The plans that took shape in my mind were bubbling up inside of me as I sat before my friends in Kafe Kabir. 'I want to start a tour company,' I began.

'Where?' Kabir asked. 'Travelling the world?'

I looked at Meera and saw a small frown cross her face before she quickly brushed it aside. I spoke quickly to reassure her that I would not go far. 'No,' I said, looking at all three faces. 'I want to start offering tours to people in India.'

'Interesting,' Nisha mused. 'But do people really want to take a tour in their own country? I thought they usually travelled to different places of the world.'

'That's the thing,' I explained. 'Too often we take our own country and its amazing culture for granted. I did the same thing when I met you all. I was always keen to run to other places... New York, Paris, places in Canada.

'But India always called me home. And now that I've been travelling around the country to places both known and unknown, I realised that I could do something that no one else has.'

'And what is that?' Meera asked, curiosity dancing in her eyes. I reached out and held her hand.

'Think about this,' I continued. 'When you travel, how do you do it? You go to a hotel, take out a guidebook, and take day trips to the places that the writers direct you to. You are one of a hundred, or a thousand, walking that same path.

'And at the end of the day, you go back to your hotel, think about your day, and plan for the next day.'

'What do you propose then?' Kabir asked, lacing his fingers together. He started to lean forward over the table and I wondered absently if it was because he was concentrating on what I was saying, or if it was so he could hear me better over the din of the café.

'I want to take small groups. I want to arrange for them to stay in people's houses, immersed in the culture. Not in a hotel room with the same walls and the same slightly uncomfortable bed that they were in the day before.

'Have you ever gone to a strange place and wondered what the local people eat? Where they go when they take their families on picnics?'

My friends nodded, and I could see the excitement lighting up their eyes as they started to understand and feel my passion. In turn, my own eagerness started to multiply, and I could feel the smile lighting up my eyes as I continued.

'Take our own city, for example,' I said. 'There is so much to do and see in Pune. But a traveller might be so overwhelmed by all the traffic and the movement in the city that they might not know how to truly enjoy their visit. Or, what if they only know to go to the popular tourist areas? All our temples, the zoo and some of the parks?'

Meera nodded thoughtfully. 'It would be like seeing the surface of a lake. Underneath the surface is a whole other world, a complex ecosystem. But if you didn't know to look there, you would miss so much.'

'Exactly!' I said. 'And there is so much information we can share. For example, people might decide to visit the Torna Fort, but they might not realise that it can take a couple hours to climb up to view it and that there is no place to buy water at the top, so they should bring their own.'

Nisha nudged Kabir. 'I seem to recall that happening to us once. Where were we? I can't remember.'

Kabir threw his head back and laughed heartily. 'Lohagad Fort; how could you forget?'

Meera and I watched the couple exchanging words, and then I gently brought the conversation back to my discussion. 'Those are exactly the things that a company like mine could do and bring value to travellers,' I said. 'A write-up on a website greatly differs from going with someone who has those bits of information. But it can go beyond the basics as well. If you're going to Rajgad Fort, you can find important information on any smartphone, but there is so much more than what someone is going to read in a few paragraphs on a website.'

'Such as?' Nisha prodded.

I was happy to have her challenging me. Nisha had an amazing way of prodding people to reach further in what they were doing. It must have been the mother in her. 'Such as... I can provide a detailed history of the fort.'

'History is critical for people, although many don't realise it,' Meera said thoughtfully. 'It explains why people do what they do... and why they made the decisions they did to shape our country.'

Although it was very hot in the café and I could feel my shirt clinging to me a little, I shivered. Meera completely understood my ambition. I squeezed her hand once again; I was so happy that she was thinking the same way I was.

'I think it's the perfect idea,' Meera said, giving me a huge grin.

'I do, too,' Kabir agreed. 'So, have you decided on a name yet?'

I nodded. 'I will call it "Musafir".'

Nisha grinned. '"Traveller"—I love it!'

Meera and Kabir nodded their agreement. 'It's the perfect name, Vivaan,' Meera breathed.

'I am so happy for you, my friend,' Kabir said sincerely. 'You are meant for amazing things, and what a perfect way to show people our country. You will be flying even higher than ever.'

I looked at my friends. I had known they would support me, but I was humbled by their encouragement.

'What are the next steps?' Meera asked.

'I'll be meeting some investors in Bangalore who might be interested in contributing to my startup,' I said. 'It will be on a small scale at first until I grow the business, but I think people will be interested in the concept.'

'Terrific!' Meera said enthusiastically. 'When will these meetings take place?'

'I haven't confirmed anything yet,' I said. 'It was important for me to discuss the idea with you three first. But I'm thinking sometime next week.' I turned to Meera. 'Do you think you would be able to come with me? We could have a small holiday together between my meetings with the investors.'

'Let me check.' Meera frowned a little, thinking. She reached into her purse, pulled out her phone, and began to check her schedule. 'Oh,' she said, disappointment in her voice. 'That is when the Delhi Lit Fest is scheduled. But this is important. I can cancel my meetings and come with you.'

I shook my head. 'No, no,' I said. 'That is an important time for you as well.'

'But I want to support you,' she insisted, a look of determination flashing in her eyes.

'We are both following our dreams,' I said. 'This is only one step in both of our careers, but it is an important one for each of us.'

Meera smiled and leaned over for a small hug. 'That is a very good point,' she said. 'We will have plenty of opportunities to do things together.'

'It's all settled, then,' Kabir said happily, clapping his hands loudly. 'Let's get back to our guests and let Jianna open her presents.'

We stood up from the small table and watched Kabir and Nisha return to the party. Meera started to follow them, but I caught her hand and tugged her close to my side. Burying my face in her hair, I said quietly, 'Let's plan a special dinner date this weekend. You and I need some alone time to celebrate before we go off on our respective trips.'

Meera leaned into my arms and I could feel her nodding. 'I think that is a very good idea,' she murmured her agreement.

Although my thoughts were bursting with ideas for Musafir, another idea was starting to move to the front of my mind. Meera and I had been together for three years now, and while we had both decided to take our relationship slowly, I was beginning to think it was time to take things to the next level. I knew she was the woman I wanted to spend the rest of my life with. Without a doubt, I knew I was ready to ask Meera to marry me.

5

VIVAAN

Meera's black high-heeled shoes clicked smartly on the tiled floor as we walked to the entrance of the rooftop restaurant. Although firmly beside her, my thoughts were still at her house as I relived picking her up.

Once again, she took my breath away when she answered the door. Her hair flowed loosely over her shoulders, and there was a soft curl in her dark tresses. Her dress was black and hugged her thin body beautifully, as if, it too was as taken with her beauty as I was.

'You look amazing,' I heard myself say, so taken with her appearance that I barely realised the words came past my lips. 'Amazing' was such an understatement, but I wasn't equipped to truly put words to my feelings. She was almost too perfect to touch.

Then she broke into her beautiful Meera smile and threw her arms around me, giving me an excited hug. 'You did tell me to dress up,' she said happily. 'Although you still haven't told me where we are going.'

'It's a surprise,' I said, still astonished myself that I had managed to secure a reservation at Paasha, one of the most popular restaurants in Pune.

And now, we were at that restaurant, its glass columns glowing with a soft green light as we walked to the entrance. 'I can't believe you got reservations here,' she whispered excitedly. 'I have always wanted to come here!'

I nodded modestly. It was the perfect place to take her, knowing I wanted to talk to her about our future together.

The air was warm as we were escorted to our table, and I heard Meera squeal a little as we took in the beautiful city now waking up for the night. The traffic noises were far below us, and barely noticeable over the soft music.

I saw Meera's eyebrows rise when I ordered a bottle of Sutter Home Fre Brut—her favourite non-alcoholic champagne. When we were alone again, she leaned across the table and whispered, 'Gorgeous rooftop view, expensive champagne... this is a wonderful way to celebrate Musafir.'

I started to speak but she leaned back, her eyes dancing in the soft lights. 'I haven't been able to stop thinking about it, to be honest,' she continued. 'I think it is such a wonderful idea. I love travelling with you because you take the time to learn about where we are going and when we are there, you thoughtfully offer information, not because you know so much, but because you genuinely want to share your knowledge.'

'I'm so glad you understand that about me,' I said. It was exactly what I try to do... to entertain and educate, but not in an 'I know more than you' type of way.

'I do,' she gushed. 'The natural next step for you is to start your own tour company.'

'I really can't wait,' I said. 'I've been thinking about it for a while. But now that I've talked to you about the idea, now that I've put the words out there in the air and spoken them out loud, suddenly, I can't get it started fast enough!'

'Good. Then do it.' She crossed her arms like she was challenging me.

'Yes, ma'am,' I said, giving her a playful salute. 'And how is your writing going?'

Her face fell just a little bit. 'Okay, I guess.'

I felt my eyebrows rise. That wasn't like Meera. 'Okay? You guess?'

She rolled her eyes and shook her head before giving me a beautiful smile. 'Just a little bit of writer's block or something,' she said. 'No big deal. I'm just trying to figure out the next step I want to take.'

'Anything you want to talk over? Maybe I can help.'

'I'm sure this is just a little hiccup,' she said, taking another sip of the champagne. 'I just kind of feel like the path I started on with this one storyline is not the right one. I'm thinking of just deleting it and starting over with that section.'

'Isn't that hard?' I asked. 'If you've put so much work into something, won't it be hard to just make it go away?'

Meera shrugged her slender shoulders. 'Perhaps. But if it isn't right, it isn't right.'

We slid into a comfortable silence for a few minutes and then I pressed on to my next topic. The reason we were really here.

'Actually, Meera,' I began a little nervously, 'I wanted to talk to you about something else.'

Surprise washed across her face. 'Really?'

I grinned at her confusion. 'Yes. There is something else I wanted to discuss with you.'

She lifted her beautiful shoulders in a shrug. 'Well, okay,' she said. 'I'll admit, I'm a little surprised. I thought we were just going to brainstorm ideas about Musafir. What is it you wanted to discuss?'

I didn't know where to start. As much as I had practised the words over and over again in my head, nothing would come out.

Sensing my nervousness, Meera said my name gently. 'What's wrong?' she said, her voice rising a little with concern.

I cleared my throat. *This is ridiculous*, I thought. *We've been together for three years. It's a big move, but she is my best friend, and the woman I know I want to spend the rest of my life with*. So why did this feel so odd?

Meera immediately narrowed her eyes, piercing me with her questioning stare. 'Where are you, Vivaan? You seem a million miles away right now. You're not planning on running again, are you?'

I let out a laugh. 'No! Believe me, Meera, that is the last thing I'm thinking about,' I assured her. I reached across the table and laced my fingers with hers.

She let out a relieved sigh. 'I'm sorry I even thought it,' she said. 'You just seem so—'

'Marriage,' I said, interrupting her when I blurted out the word. 'What do you think about the idea of getting married? Some day?'

Her eyes grew wide as my words washed over her. 'Vivaan,' she said. 'What exactly are you saying?'

I cleared my throat again. 'Well,' I began. 'We've been together for a long time now.'

'Three years,' she confirmed.

'Yes,' I said. 'Over the last three years, we have shared a lot. But we've also been apart a lot. Your career is just starting, and you've had to put a tremendous amount of time into it. And I'm glad,' I said quickly, afraid she would think I was complaining. 'You knew what you wanted in life, you knew you wanted to be a writer, and you made it happen. I am so proud of you.

'And while you've been going off to book signings and other commitments with your writing, I've been going in my own directions, travelling and learning more about where we live.'

'Yes, that is true,' Meera agreed.

'I'm just thinking that maybe if we were married, our relationship would be more stable. We could still go off and do what we love, but we would always know we were coming home to each other.'

Meera sat back and chewed on her lip thoughtfully.

'I don't have a ring or anything,' I said. 'I just thought we should talk about it for now. See if this is the next logical step for us.'

I waited and watched Meera take a deep breath. And then another. I could see her thinking hard, but it was one of those rare times that I had no idea what was in her mind. Her eyes drifted away from mine, taking in Pune at night but I had a feeling she was barely seeing what was in front of her.

Finally, I couldn't take it any longer. 'Meera, say something...'

'Well,' she began slowly, twirling the stem of her glass between her fingers. 'I'm just surprised.'

'You are?' I asked. 'But we've been together for three years.'

Meera nodded. 'And it's been a wonderful three years with you.'

'And this is the logical next step,' I prodded.

Taking another sip, she gently put the glass on the table and reached for me, wrapping both of her soft hands around mine. 'In a lot of ways, yes. But, Vivaan, you surprised me because I never really thought it was possible with us.'

'Why not?'

'Radha,' she said simply.

Even after all this time, hearing her name made my stomach lurch. Radha, the woman I was going to marry, was murdered on our wedding day. It broke me so deeply that I never thought I would be able to fully heal.

I looked in Meera's eyes and remembered the day I told her about Radha. I watched Meera's hopes for a future with me crumble as I confessed that I would never be able to love her the way I had loved my fiancée and that my heart was still committed to another woman, one long dead.

Although I was always the one running away early in our relationship, that day Meera ran from me. She ended up on the path to Chor Darwaja and fell down the steep slope at Rajgad. For days, she was in a coma.

'I don't know if you heard me while you were in the

coma, Meera, but even then, I was telling you that my heart had found its home with you. I loved you then and I love you now. You, Meera, are not someone in my life who replaced Radha in my heart. You are your own person. You are strong, wonderful, kind, caring.

'You are you. You are my Meera.'

Tears glistened in her eyes as she absorbed my words.

We ate in relative silence, speaking only to make small talk over our delicious meal. At first, I was afraid that I had ruined our evening, but watching Meera's delight as she ate her palak paneer, and then how she playfully took a bit of the dal paasha from my spoon, I knew her silence was because she was negotiating through a maze of confusion at my talk of marriage.

I truly had no idea that she had dismissed the idea of marrying me because of Radha, but I vowed to make Meera understand that she was the most important woman in my life.

'Vivaan,' Meera started after we shared a delicious dessert of phirni, 'I'm sorry that I've been so quiet about what you were saying. You surprised me but I do know you love me. And I love you too. This is just a new idea for me to absorb.'

'I understand,' I said, relieved that she was considering the idea.

'Let's take some time and think about it,' she suggested. 'You go on your trip to Bangalore and I'll go to the Delhi Lit Fest as planned. When those are behind us, let's talk about the idea some more.'

That night, as we said goodbye, I could feel her love like a burst of energy as she kissed me goodnight. I knew that although I had caught her off guard, she was not rejecting me, or turning away from our love. She simply needed some time to acclimate herself to something she had thought was an impossibility for us.

6
FATE

We see inspiration all the time, on a warm day after a week of rain, in watching a parent bird feed its baby, in the laughter of a loved one.

It doesn't need to be something concrete. But, on the other hand, it can be someone giving you a piece of advice or challenging you to push yourself a little harder. Take that limit that you can see in front of you and plan to take one step beyond it. And then another, and another.

Inspiration is that bird learning how to fly. It can sit in its nest every day from the moment it hatches, and watch its parents flying to and fro. That baby bird will then practise, standing in the nest and unfurling its wings, feeling the breeze weaving through its new feathers. It will take some tentative flaps, feeling its toes lifting away from that safe and secure home.

But one day, it needs to stop pretending and throw itself out of the nest, flapping its wings furiously, its heart pounding in its breast.

That is how people garner courage when they are inspired. They take chances.

That baby bird can't stop flying though. When there is no nest under it, it can't just stop flapping its wings or it will go crashing to the earth.

Sometimes, I'm not content to just watch people take flight and follow their dreams.

Yes, life is about inspiration, but it's also about struggle.

After all, you can't appreciate the sweet nectar of life without a little vinegar of challenges.

How boring life would be if people just moved

throughout the day, thriving in the monotony of their day. Work. Family. A little bit of fun, maybe. Or maybe not. Some people really don't know how to have fun… all they know is how to keep their head down, not make any waves, and just churn through life.

That, to them, is what a 'good life' is all about.

They are utter fools if you ask me. That isn't a good life; that's just plain boring.

Oh no, it's about taking your hand and smacking the top of the water, forcing the ripples into otherwise smooth sailing. It's about the struggle.

Struggles are what keep people on their toes.

7

MEERA

The colours were amazing. Everywhere I turned, there was something new to take in at Dilli Haat, where the Delhi Lit Fest was being held. Banners, flags, clothing, it was amazing to me.

The colours were a good analogy for my own feelings, I thought with some humour. I was so excited to be here; since my early days of wanting to become a professional writer, I dreamed of being here. I was also a little nervous. Writers should be used to criticism, but sometimes it was hard to shake off a particularly stinging critique. There was a little confusion as I navigated between the music and the workshops, but there was also a feeling of satisfaction. I belonged here, at this place, surrounded by people who had similar goals and dreams. My peers, I thought happily.

As all those different hues and sensations circled me and wove their way through my mind, I found that even the brightest colours are tinted with a tendril of confusion. No matter where I was in my day or what I was doing, the idea of marrying Vivaan was always present.

From the first moments I laid eyes on my traveller, I was taken by Vivaan; even before I knew his name. I saw him first at Coffee & Us, where I had gone to listen to various authors and poets. Vivaan was there, but it took forever for us to connect until I convinced Kabir to text me the next time he showed up at the café.

Bold? Perhaps, but he had captured my attention before we even spoke two words to each other.

Consequently, a relationship with him was a dream come true, and the past years with him had been everything I could have wanted. Even when we were apart physically, I knew we were always connected emotionally.

So, why was I so confused when he mentioned marriage? My first thought was of his fiancée and how he told me so long ago that his feelings toward me could never be the same as his love for her.

But as I thought about it later, there was more to my hesitation than just Radha. It was time to be honest with myself. Was I ready for this next step?

With my first session at the festival behind me, I was ready to take a few minutes to have some water and give way to all my thoughts. But there were so many people and I found myself jostled in the crowds in my drive to seek a bit of solitude.

I bumped into a strong shoulder. 'I am so sorry,' I began before my eyes even met his.

'It's quite… Meera!'

'Arjun! I wondered if I might see you here,' I said with delight as it registered that I literally ran into my mentor, the man who inspired me to take the step and become a writer.

'I would never miss it,' Arjun Mehra said, giving me an enthusiastic hug. 'It is great to see you. You look fantastic.'

I pulled back and took a good look at him, smiling hugely. 'Thank you,' I said. 'You look well, too. You haven't changed a bit.'

He laughed and rolled his eyes. 'Except for all the grey hairs.'

I barked out a laugh of my own. 'Barely,' I said as I pretended to study the distinguished grey at his temples. 'Well,' I teased. 'One or two, perhaps.'

'It's so nice to see you… you are a fresh breeze in this crowded place,' he said. 'Where do you go next?'

'Just going to take a break,' I said. 'And you?'

'Nothing that can't be rescheduled,' Arjun decided.

'Let's go catch up somewhere. I want you to fill me in on everything. It's been too long.'

He held out his arm in greeting and I happily linked my arm with his. Together, we navigated the crowds until the people thinned out and we found a relatively quiet place to sit.

He reached into his satchel and pulled out two bottles of water, handing one to me. 'It's a little warm, but it's better than nothing,' he decided.

I cracked the top off my bottle, and we clicked the plastic together in a toast. It may have been only water, but it felt delicious on a hot day. 'Just what I needed,' I pronounced. 'Thank you.'

'You can thank me by telling me all about the gang at Kafe Kabir. How are Kabir and Nisha? And the baby?'

'Everyone is doing very well,' I said, slipping into the comfortable task of providing updates on everyone. I loved filling him in with Jianna's tales. 'The darling, even though she hasn't mastered walking, is already taken with clothes. Nisha's family sent her a box of hand-me-downs a few weeks ago. She spent an hour—a whole hour—peeling off clothes and pulling on new ones. She was like some princess trying on new ball gowns,' I laughed. 'And shoes... she is forever stealing other people's shoes.'

Arjun's laughter matched my own. 'I can't wait to get back to Pune and meet this sweetheart,' he said. 'I'll have to make it soon before she grows too much more.'

'Bring her a new outfit,' I suggested. 'She will adore you forever.'

'I shall do that,' he determined, before abruptly changing the subject. 'And Vivaan? How are you two doing?' Despite my best attempt to mask my confusion, a sigh escaped. 'Is everything okay?' Arjun asked softly.

'It is,' I said. 'We're just reaching a bit of a turning point in our relationship and I have a lot on my mind.' I leaned back and let my eyes wander to the colourful banners swaying in the gentle, warm breeze.

'Ah. A "turning point". So... he has proposed then?' I watched his face split into a slightly impish grin, like a happy big brother. 'He's a good man; I admire his dedication a lot. And'—he cleared his throat rather dramatically—'he has fantastic taste ... I mean, not only is he with you, but, if I recall, one of his first gifts to you was an autographed copy of my book!'

My raw nerves shattered into a relieved laugh; my mentor joined in. It felt like a weight was lifted off of my shoulders ... temporarily. But then it settled back down heavily.

I sighed again. 'Can I be candid?' I asked.

'But of course, Meera. You are a wise woman, and I would be honoured if you felt you could trust me enough to be honest with me.'

I reached down and picked at a stray weed that marred the grassy patch we were sitting on. 'I truly appreciate that, Arjun.' I ran the weed through my fingers, trying to decide how to broach the subject.

With the insight of a writer, he seemed to easily surmise my quandary. 'It's the...' I started, trying to find the right words. 'Not proposal. He didn't ask me to marry him, not with a ring.'

'No?'

'No.'

'But he brought up the subject, I'm guessing,' Arjun surmised.

I nodded miserably. 'Yes, he did.'

'Tell me more,' he suggested gently. 'If you want to, of course. I certainly wouldn't want to pry. I try not to pry, but I think that is something we writers always struggle with. We want to expose the truth, the raw emotions, don't you think?'

I chuckled at his insights. 'It's complicated, I'm afraid. I'm only just wrapping my head around the whole thing, and I'm afraid there is much more to it.'

'Because of the woman he was going to marry.'

'Mostly,' I said, before adjusting my response. 'Not mostly. Partly. When he told me about Radha, it nearly broke my heart. The moment he mentioned her name, I felt there was a great spirit that rose between us. It had obviously been there at the time, I just didn't realise what it was then. His love didn't die when she did; I knew that as soon as he said her name.

'That was when I ran,' I admitted.

'To Rajgad Fort,' he confirmed.

My head dropped in defeat. 'Yes.'

'But, Meera, that was long before he met you.' Although he had been sitting back in a relaxed posture, he now sat up again, his attention on me.

I squirmed. 'It was,' I said.

'And after that, did his feelings change?'

'Yes,' I whispered.

As if sensing his unblinking gaze directed at me was making me uncomfortable, his eyes left mine and I watched his attention sweep over the people who walked by. I found myself relaxing a little more and I took another big gulp of water.

'Tell me how things are now,' he suggested.

My thoughts danced wildly over the past few years. They waltzed with our embraces, some passionate, others more familiar, warm and comfortable. Of course, we had disagreements, as did any couple, but they were minor and thinking of them now, I could barely discern the catalyst for an argument.

'Things are good,' I confirmed. 'Very, very good. I am so very happy, with my life, with my work, and especially with Vivaan.'

'Then what is wrong?'

His questions, though short and concise, were like signposts, guiding my reasoning to the real crux of the matter. As if with a sharp knife, he was carefully peeling away the thin layers of excuses and arguments. I realised this as my thoughts were drawn full circle to the real matter at hand.

'I think maybe they are too good,' I began slowly as realisation emerged. 'What I mean is, I have my career and Vivaan has his. He is in the process of starting his own travel company and is very excited about the niche concept he has developed.

'Our relationship is strong as it is right now. If we get married, that will change. What he thinks will give us a solid foundation for coming back to each other...,' I turned worried eyes to his. 'What if that ties us down instead of giving us the freedom to follow our dreams? Marriage would take away a degree of freedom that we both have.'

Arjun drew his knees up and rested his elbows on them. 'Do you really think your relationship and your freedom would be compromised by marriage? I can't imagine either of you letting this tie you down. You love each other.'

'Of course.'

'That, Meera, will not change. Even if you and Vivaan are going in different directions physically, emotionally, and spiritually, you are both travelling the same path, side by side.'

'And marriage would make that stronger...'

'In your case, with Vivaan, I think so.' Arjun stopped and then spoke in a mock-stern voice. 'Here is my disclaimer. I'm not a fortune teller so I can't promise you either direction will make you happy for the rest of your life.' He leaned toward me and nudged my shoulder playfully as his voice brightened again. 'But I don't think running from the idea is a good idea. Talk to Vivaan, Meera. Tell him your hesitation. Be honest with him... and yourself.'

I smiled as his words began to sink in. 'You are a wise man, Arjun,' I said.

'And a cheap therapist, too,' he teased.

I felt a frown teasing my forehead once again. 'Tell me, do you think I am wrong to question this? It's no secret that Vivaan is the man of my dreams. He is good to me and he makes me deliriously happy. Do you think I'm crazy to question marrying him?'

'No,' he said seriously. 'In fact, I am most encouraged by the fact that you are questioning this next step. To do so, you're thinking with all your heart, your soul, and your head. You're not blindly following your heart, and you're not letting your head drive you in a specific direction. You are most wise, my friend. And that, I am sure, will lead you to the best conclusion for both you and Vivaan.'

'Arjun, thank you,' I said, feeling that for the first time in days, I was breathing clean, uncluttered air. It wasn't that Vivaan's suggestion was a bad one, not at all. But the pressure I immediately felt from the idea of 'happily ever after' weighing on me—innocently, but heavily—fell away, dissolving with the antidote of reason.

'Don't thank me,' he said, his eyes flaming in their desire to help. 'If my ramblings can help you, I am more than happy to assist, my friend. Please, let me know how things are going with—'

'Meera,' my assistant called to me, interrupting Arjun. I looked up to see her pushing through the crowds. 'There you are! I tried calling but there wasn't an answer on your phone.'

Sheepishly, I dug my phone out and saw several missed calls. 'I am so sorry, Aashi. I didn't even notice...'

'It's okay,' she responded, her voice still harried from rushing through the crowds. 'It's time to meet your publishers, though.'

'Oh!' Arjun said, pushing himself off the grass and reaching out quickly to help me to my feet. How the man could move so fast was beyond me, but he had more energy than a kitten. 'Off with you! No matter where life takes you, no matter how far you are from your home, I hope your journeys always serve to keep you two close.'

We shared a quick goodbye hug and I thanked him again before Aashi and I disappeared back into the tidal wave of the now-growing crowds.

'You'll make it if we hurry,' Aashi said reassuringly. 'Luckily the hotel is so close.'

My phone vibrated in my hand, the ringtone drowned among all the voices around me. Frowning, I looked at the screen. 'It's Nisha,' I said, then decided, 'I'll have to call her back.'

We were waiting for a break in the traffic when the phone rang again. Once more, it was Nisha. 'It must be important,' I said to Aashi. 'She knows I'm at the festival.'

Aashi took my belongings so I could answer the call. I swiped the phone and pressed my other hand over my ear so I could hear her better. 'Nisha. Is everything okay?'

All I could hear was sobbing on the other side.

'Nisha!' I said again, startled. 'Calm down so I can hear you! What is wrong?' I looked over at Aashi, a horrible feeling washing over me.

Between the sobs, I could hear deep breaths as my friend tried to pull herself together.

'It's Kabir,' she said finally.

'Kabir? What happened?' Now I was terrified. Something happened. Something bad. My thoughts went everywhere but my focus was on the phone as I felt Aashi guiding me through the milling crowds.

'There's been an… accident.' Nisha continued. 'There… was…' She sobbed again. 'A fire at the café.'

'No!' I said, horrified. 'Is Kabir okay?'

'I don't know,' she said. 'He was burned badly. He was rushed to the hospital and I am waiting for the doctors right now. Oh Meera, I'm so scared!'

'He'll be okay,' I tried to reason. 'He's strong.'

'Can you come back to Pune?'

I looked over at Aashi, who was already wrestling all my belongings on one arm so she could pull out her own phone, ready to make calls.

'Of course,' I said. 'I'll get there as soon as I can.'

Barely having pulled herself together enough to speak to me, I could hear Nisha begin sobbing, out of control again. 'Thank…' she began before breaking off into another sob.

'I'll be there as soon as I can,' I said. 'Which hospital?'

'Siddharth Hospital,' she responded. 'He'll be in the burns ICU.'

'I'll see you soon,' I promised and hung up.

I began to jog through the crowded sidewalk, Aashi rushing to keeping up with me. 'Kabir is in ICU,' I said. 'There's been a fire. I have to go.'

'Of course,' Aashi said. 'You go pack. I'll call the publishers and explain there has been an emergency. Then I'll book you on the next flight to Pune.'

I turned grateful eyes to my assistant. 'Thank you.'

She nodded soberly. 'Are you okay, Meera?' she asked.

Was I okay? I wasn't crying, but I could feel the adrenaline racing through my veins. 'I think I'm numb right now,' I said as we reached the hotel. 'Just get me on the first possible plane so I can get home.'

8

VIVAAN

As busy as the traffic can be in Pune, the vehicles darting in and out of the roads in Bangalore never ceased to amaze me. They were like bees buzzing around to defend their hives from an invading bear ... all moving in singular directions but with an urgency as a whole entity to get to the next point.

Despite getting a good night's sleep in my modest hotel, I was still exhausted. Thoughts of Meera invaded my mind, like a weighted-down vest clinging to every synapse. I was still surprised at her hesitation when I brought up marriage last week.

The confusion tugged at her beautiful smile and at once, I was afraid I had made a horrible mistake. Was the idea of taking our relationship to the next step going to ultimately be a wedge between us? As I replayed the evening, my mind worked through the words we spoke, gliding over her encouraging ones and stopping at her hesitant, puzzled questions like a brush snags on a lock of tangled hair.

I shook my head, forcing my concerns out of my head. I knew Meera loved me. Her heart and soul sparkled with the rays of love, becoming more pronounced as we built memories together over these many months. I knew she was the woman I would spend the rest of my life with, knew it with determined certainty.

It was time to set aside any negative thoughts and direct my mind toward positive ones, kindling my confidence for the hours ahead.

Today was an important day for me. Today was the day I would be meeting possible investors to convince them of my dream to open Musafir. I believed in my dream as much as I believed in my love for Meera, and I was sure that this confidence would translate to several successful meetings.

Soon, oh so soon, Musafir would be more than just the thoughts in my mind. Soon, it would be the avenue people would take to learn more about our beautiful country. I really couldn't wait—surely, someone would see the value of my idea and help me breathe life into my dream.

Finishing my breakfast, I picked up my phone to start looking for an Uber to bring me to my destination. Even though it was a quick flight, I was tired by the time I landed, and so had decided to book a hotel near the airport. I knew that meant it would be about an hour from there to meet with my investors, but it was worth it for me to get to bed soon.

I looked through the app and was disappointed to find that there weren't any vehicles close to my location. I couldn't afford to be picky right now. I needed to leave soon so I could get started on my first round of meetings. I began looking for shared rides on my app.

Finding one close by, I reserved the ride and quickly gathered my belongings, leaving payment for my meal on the table. Rushing out of the restaurant, I caught my server's eye and nodded towards my table to let her know that I had left the money behind.

It was already warm when I stepped outside; the air clogged with heat and dust. Anxiously, I waited near the narrow street for my ride to appear.

When it did, I climbed into the cab, gave my destination to the driver and nodded to the other gentleman beside me. He was younger than me; his eyes had a sharp, intelligent look and his clothes were neatly pressed. He was obviously on his way to work.

I settled my belongings and introduced myself.

'I'm Parth,' he said, holding out his hand to shake mine.

'Where are you going today?' I asked.

At that, I saw his shoulders droop a little bit as he sighed deeply. 'To work,' he said simply.

I knew that look; it was very similar to the one I had when I used to work at the bank. It said he was determined to have a productive day, but that he wasn't going to enjoy it at all. I nodded sympathetically.

'What do you do for work?' I asked, curious.

'I'm a marketing manager for one of the dot-com companies in Bangalore. The company has been around for quite a while but there is a lot of competition and my company is demanding more and more of me to attract more business.'

I groaned, understanding his frustration. 'I completely understand. No matter how well you do, no matter how much business you attract, your company sees that as a reason to push harder and harder.'

'Exactly,' he agreed. 'If I brought in 100 customers this month, why can't I bring in 110 next month? Or, heaven forbid, if I attract less than that 100 customers next month!'

'How long have you been with your company?'

'Two years. Two very long years. Don't get me wrong, they are good to me,' he said quickly so I knew he was not disparaging his company. 'I make a good salary and there are plenty of opportunities to direct my own creativity. It's just that... ,' he broke off, suddenly lost in his thoughts.

I continued for him, knowing his story well. 'It's just that they want you to keep doing more.'

'Yes.'

We sat in silence for a little while before Parth spoke again. 'Where are you going today, Vivaan?'

I smiled, excited once more at the prospect of the day. 'I am actually on my way to meeting some potential investors for a company I am trying to start up.'

'That is fantastic,' my companion said, his eyes lighting up. 'What kind of company do you want to have? Another software company?' he guessed.

I shook my head and laughed. 'No, nothing like that,' I responded. I looked out of the dusty window, but my mind was suddenly in the rich, green jungles of Satpura National Park. In my memory, I was climbing up from a steep valley, after having climbed down to a river to watch otters frolicking in the late morning sun. My shoes dug into the damp earth as I ascended the steep path all around me, I heard the sounds of wildlife; the high-pitched screech of the spotted eagle, the rumblings of large mammals. It was exhilarating and as my attention returned to my current setting, I brought back a handful of that green peace with me.

I told Parth that I was going to start a unique tour company.

'To other countries?' he asked, curious.

'No,' I smiled, easing into my concept once more. 'It will be a company that organises trips in India.'

Parth pursed his lips and thought about it. 'But there are similar companies here, aren't there?'

'Not like this,' I said. I wanted to tell him more, but I had only just met the young man and I decided to keep the specifics close for now. Something told me I could trust him, but I knew how quickly an idea could be let out, even if it was accidental. He could be excited and tell a peer at work, who might tell someone else... and before you know it, there would be a handful of Musafirs I would be competing with. No, better to keep the crux of the idea to myself for now ... well, except for my friends and the investors I hoped to convince.

'I understand,' Parth said. 'If it's a good idea, you should keep it to yourself for now. I've had dreams of starting my own company as well,' he added. 'I would be devastated if

I finally made that move and left my predictable income to chase a dream that wasn't so special, after all.'

'You're not happy with your current job, then?' I asked, eager to turn the conversation away from my own startup. I loved talking about it, but I had to remind myself that although I instinctively knew I could trust my companion, he was still a stranger. I needed to be careful; I shouldn't talk too much about the company before it had even started.

He shook his head. 'Again, it is a good position for me, and I worked hard to get there, but no. I am not happy. I dream of being my own person, answering only to myself, following my own dreams.'

'So, why not do it?' I asked.

Parth smiled sadly. 'Because what if I fail?'

'But what if you succeeded?' I asked hypothetically. 'You would never know how far your dreams can take you until you take that first step.'

'You make it sound so easy,' he responded. 'You have so much confidence. But what if *you* fail?' Suddenly he stopped and blushed. 'I am sorry, Vivaan. I didn't mean to be negative. You seem so sure and it is wrong of me to put my own caution on your dreams. I hope I have not offended you!'

I laughed. 'I am not offended,' I said, giving him a big grin to reassure him that I was not put off by his comments. 'You are right; it is hard to take chances sometimes. May I share a story with you?'

Parth nodded and sat back in the well-used seat, sighing in relief. 'Absolutely.'

'I was like you once,' I began, thinking of my own misery when I worked at the bank. I could feel its oppression weighing on me like a heavy foot pressing down on my head, trying to push me to the ground. 'I had a great job, one that was full of promise. I had money and could afford the nicest home. But, despite all the security, all the new things around me, I was miserable.'

'I can definitely relate to that,' Parth said, nodding earnestly.

'It is easy to be trapped into that feeling of security, isn't it? But notice I used the word "trapped" and "security" in the same sentence. It is good to know that you are in a secure career, but for many like me—and I think like you—our spirits are not meant to sit behind a desk, scurrying to make a healthy bottom line financially for our company. There is so much more to life.'

'I suppose so. And you've been happy?' he asked curiously.

'Well,' I admitted, 'there had been struggles along the way as my own story started to reroute itself. But I was able to open myself up to other very good things. Like Meera.'

'Meera,' Parth repeated her name as if he realised how important she was to me.

I nodded. 'Meera was in the process of following her own dream. She wanted to become a writer. That was why she was at the café that night.'

'So, love at first sight?' he teased, tapping his fingers together in anticipation.

I shrugged. 'If I had allowed it to, probably. But I was in the process of escaping at that point and it wasn't until later that we became a couple.'

'And Meera is a writer?'

I nodded proudly. 'Meera pursued her dreams and has an amazing career. She's published two books already and she's India's highest selling female author right now,' I said.

'Truly?' Parth said. 'What has she written?'

'Her first book was called *Everyone Has a Story*.'

His eyes lit up. 'Oh! I read that. Yes, it's a very inspiring story … but that only really happens in stories.'

I shook my head earnestly. 'No. It's all true. It captures my story with hers and that of our very good friends. It is very much how it happened.'

He looked at me, his eyes wide. 'Seriously?' he asked, awe and hope in his voice.

'Seriously.'

'I'm so amazed. I still can't believe this. And all this because you all took chances and pursued your own hopes, dreams, and desires,' Parth said, nodding thoughtfully.

'Yes,' I said.

'But,' Parth started again. 'What if you failed? Or what if Meera or Kabir failed?'

'Let me ask you this,' I said, knowing that we were coming close to my destination. 'What if they hadn't tried? What if I stayed with my company?'

'You would be living a life of regret,' he responded quietly.

'Exactly. Kabir and Nisha wouldn't be together, Meera wouldn't have her novels. And I would be sitting behind a desk every day, staring at an endless stream of numbers.' I couldn't help shuddering a bit at the idea. 'It's okay to fail,' I said earnestly, 'but it is far worse to live an unfulfilled life of regret. To always wonder where I would be, what I would be doing if I had followed my dreams and had the courage to walk out the doors of Citibank that day.'

Our Uber pulled up to my destination. I shook Parth's hand.

'Good luck today,' he said. 'And thank you for your encouraging words. Believe me, you have given me a lot to think about.'

I climbed out of the car. 'And good luck to you, too,' I said. 'I have a feeling the next time we meet, you'll have your own story to tell me!'

Parth was laughing as I closed the door and turned to the tall building where the investors were waiting for me.

Before I entered the building, I pulled out my phone and sent a quick text to Meera. 'I'm here... wish me luck! I'm going to silence my phone in the meetings, but I'll check in with you after.'

With that, I turned the ringer off on my phone, squared my shoulders, and walked into the building. I was armed with an impressive portfolio of my business plan, but just as importantly, I was also equipped with memories of the beautiful locales I had visited over the last few years ... memories that I was sure was as important to convey to my investors my idea as the numbers I had prepared.

A few hours later, I was exhausted but excited at the same time. The meetings had gone well, and the investors seemed receptive to my startup plan. While nobody committed to financial support, several of them seemed to really like the idea and promised to get back to me within the next few weeks.

Outside, I took my phone out to order an Uber back to my hotel. As soon as I looked at the screen, my heart lurched. There were eleven missed calls and even more unread texts. Something had happened.

Without even checking the call list or reading the texts, I called Meera immediately.

'Vivaan!' she cried. 'Thank God you called back!' Her voice was high and choked with tears.

'What happened, Meera?'

'Kabir's been hurt!' she sobbed. 'There was a fire at the café.'

'No!' I said, shaking my head, trying to push her words away. It couldn't be. Not Kabir! 'How badly is he hurt?'

'I'm not sure. I came back from Delhi when Nisha called... I'm on my way to the hospital right now.'

'But Kabir... what happened?'

'I don't know yet. He's in surgery.'

Mentally, I calculated the distance to the airport. 'I'll call and get the next flight back to Pune,' I promised. 'Let me know if you have any updates. I'll be there as soon as I can.'

9

MEERA

My cab finally arrived at the hospital. I looked up at the imposing building. The well-balanced, bright building façade held so many emotions—joy, fear, pain, hope, and sorrow. It was impossible to predict all the stories ensconced within the hospital walls.

Although I had been sitting in the cab for what seemed like a painfully long ride from the airport, my heart was beating fearfully.

'I'll take your bags back to your house,' Aashi promised. 'And call me if you need anything. Anything at all. I can come immediately.'

I gave her a wobbly smile of gratitude before I ran into the hospital. At the reception area, it was everything I could do not to just shout out Nisha's name, but I knew how foolish that was. She was most likely on another floor, and I would have scared everyone with my behaviour.

I rushed to a reception desk. Although there was a line of people in front of me, they saw my agitation and waved me to the front of the line. Even strangers seemed aware of my urgency, and their compassion was not lost on me.

When I gave Kabir's name, a young woman entered it into the computer and waved someone over. 'Our volunteer here can take you there,' she said, and said something to the elderly man. His eyes widened, and he hurried around the counter.

'Please, come with me,' he said, gesturing at me to follow him.

I nodded my thanks to the woman and left with the volunteer. It was obvious that, even though age had slowed down his body, he was trying to hurry. 'I'm sorry I am going slowly,' he apologised. 'But I promise, it'll be easier to lead you there instead of giving you directions and sending you off to maybe get lost.'

'Thank you,' I said, willing his aged body to move faster.

'Is this a friend or a relative?' he asked.

'A friend. A good friend,' I responded as we rushed down the bright hallway. 'There was a fire at his café. I don't know much else, except that he was rushed here and was going into surgery.'

'We have some of the finest doctors in this hospital,' he promised. 'Your friend is in very good hands, I know.'

We turned a corner, and then went down another hallway before turning around another corner—he was right; I would have gotten lost for sure—and then I heard Nisha's voice. Turning quickly to the volunteer, I thanked him before I sprinted down the rest of the hallway. She was leaning heavily on Samarth, the assistant manager of the café, but started towards me as I ran.

Nisha threw herself into my arms, crying, and I had to take a step back to catch myself. 'What do you know?' I asked.

She pulled away, tears streaming down her face. 'Nothing yet. He is in surgery right now. A nurse came out at one point and told me it would be several hours.'

'He's strong,' I told Nisha. 'He will be okay, I'm sure.'

She nodded and wiped at her eyes almost angrily. 'He will,' Nisha said with an almost feral determination. I put my arm around her and we stepped out of the hallway into the surgical waiting room. I heard a pitiful whimper and realised Jianna was sitting in a chair, her eyes wide and her bottom lip trembling.

'Oh sweetheart,' I cooed and swept her into my arms, hugging her tightly and burying my nose in her beautiful baby hair, drawing in her innocent smell like a medicine.

'I came so fast, I had to bring her with me,' Nisha said. 'She's scared to death.'

'We all are,' I said, my mind hurting to see those innocent eyes wide with confusion and fear. 'I can call Aashi and have her come get the baby,' I offered. Jianna loved my assistant, and it felt wrong to have the baby here where the sights and sounds were probably terrifying her.

Nisha breathed her relief. 'That would be perfect. She wouldn't mind?'

My phone was already in my hand. 'Of course not,' I said. 'She can take Jianna back to your apartment and get her settled in.'

The cab Aashi was in was only a few blocks away and by the time I reached the main entrance with Jianna, she was rushing through the doors. 'Thank you for coming back so quickly,' I said. 'I didn't even ask if you would mind…'

Aashi shook her head quickly. 'Of course I don't mind. I'm glad to have something to do … and you know I love this little lady,' she said affectionately, gathering Jianna into her arms.

I handed her Nisha's apartment key and gave her a few quick instructions before planting a final kiss on Jianna's head. 'Your daddy will be fine,' I told the baby, even though I knew she couldn't really understand me.

Back in the waiting room, one hour pressed into two, with no word on Kabir's condition. I sat stoically beside Nisha, not speaking, leaving her to her thoughts. I hoped they were good, pleasant memories with Kabir. My own mind was filled with prayers and unanswered questions.

I was in the cafeteria getting some food for Nisha when I heard long strides rushing to me. 'Vivaan!' I said, running to his arms, the food items forgotten.

I buried my head in his chest and felt his long arms wrap around my body. I felt reassured by his strength and allowed myself to finally start crying. 'Kabir?' he said softly.

I shook my head, then realising he probably thought the worst, I managed to choke out the words: 'Nothing yet,' before my fear took over again. I cried for the woman in the waiting room, wrapped in her own cocoon of fear, I cried for the man who must have been in agonising pain, fighting for his life. I cried for their little girl, who was hopefully sleeping by now, unaware that she might just lose her father.

I cried and cried, balling Vivaan's shirt in my fists.

He, in turn, held me, whispering soothingly. I never heard the words, but I knew he was trying to take on some of my pain.

Finally, as if a light was turned on, the tears stopped. I felt my spine straighten, and Vivaan must have, too, because his arms loosened, as if he were testing my strength, much like a parent tests their child's security when learning to swim.

I pulled back, my face coated with countless tears. Running the back of his hand across my cheeks, his eyes locked with mine. 'Okay now?' he asked gently.

I took a brave gulp past my swollen throat and nodded. Then I laughed nervously. 'Where did that come from?' I said. 'I didn't mean to fall apart like that.'

Vivaan hugged me again, resting his chin on the top of my head. I loved it when he did that. 'I'm guessing you've been very strong for our Nisha, haven't you?'

'I... I guess so.'

'I'm thinking you took a much-needed break from being the strong one, Meera,' he said, squeezing my shoulders reassuringly. 'Even if you didn't want to.'

I barked out a laugh. 'No. I didn't want to.'

'It's okay to cry, Meera. But about Kabir,' he confirmed, 'we know nothing yet, right?' I shook my head. 'Then let's reinforce those walls for a little longer and go take care of Nisha. That is what Kabir would want.'

'It is,' I agreed, swiping at the last traces of tears. I knew my eyes were puffy and my nose was probably swollen, but the tears were gone. I took Vivaan's hand, lacing my fingers through his. 'Let's go back.'

Walking back to the cafeteria counter, I remembered to retrieve Nisha's pitiful meal. 'She didn't want me to go to the restaurant for her,' I explained needlessly, holding up the dry crackers.

'Wait,' he said, pulling me back quickly, and led me over to a water dispenser. 'I think you need to slow down for a minute. Have a drink. It'll help.'

I nodded gratefully and took several long, healing gulps, feeling the cool water soothe my swollen throat.

Together, we walked back to where Nisha was sitting, wrapped in her memories. She gave a sharp cry when she saw Vivaan, but this time, he rushed to her side. Standing back, my throat tightening once more, I imagined that I was watching a very similar scene that played out down the hall when I dissolved into his arms.

When Nisha's torrent of tears subsided, the two sat down, Vivaan holding her hand tightly. I slid into the chair beside her, so we had our dear friend sandwiched between us.

'What happened?' Vivaan asked. 'How could this happen?'

Nisha sniffled into a tissue and shook her head. 'I don't know, Vivaan. They are still investigating. It was early and, thankfully, there were no customers in the café at that time. The other staff were in the restaurant area getting ready for the day, and Kabir was back in the kitchen. Suddenly, they heard a horrible *whoosh* and Kabir shouted for them to get out. They turned back and could see the kitchen light up, but they never saw the fire.

Kabir was only a few steps behind them and got out of the building quickly. But still, he was there when the wires short-circuited, or whatever happened, and he was burned.'

'How did he get out?'

'Everyone left out the front door, but Kabir didn't follow right away. One of the staff was on his way back in when Kabir pushed through the door and fell to the ground.'

'Did they say how bad he was burned?' Vivaan had the courage to ask what I could not.

Nisha shook her head. 'They didn't know. They said he sort of wrapped himself into a cocoon like he was protecting what was burned. His face and clothes were black from the smoke, so they really couldn't tell how badly he was burned. When the ambulance came, they loaded him up quickly and took off.'

She trailed off and the three of us sat back in our chairs, one united being, giving and gathering strength from each other. Over Nisha's head, I caught Vivaan's gaze and I gave him a brave smile. Whatever happened, we would face it together.

My cheek was resting against Nisha's soft hair when the doctor finally came in, looking tired but positive.

He didn't even have to say Nisha's name. She saw him, took in his surgical robes, and went rushing toward him. 'Kabir?' she asked expectantly. Vivaan and I both hurried to her side, grasping her hands, maybe to keep her grounded or maybe to use them to ground us. I wasn't sure.

The surgeon nodded, a weary smile on his face. 'He is alive and stable,' he said to Nisha. 'Of course, when we go into a situation like this, we never really know how bad the injury is. Your husband had some serious damage, but he was also very lucky in that he instinctually pulled away from the fire. His quick reflexes preserved a lot of tissue that may have otherwise been even more seriously burned.'

Nisha let out a relieved cry. In response, we pulled at her, relieved and empowered at the same time. Where only a few minutes ago we were exhausted, we were all now rejuvenated and exhilarated.

'The burns are bad, though,' he warned. 'We did have to take his undamaged skin and graft them onto the badly burned parts... his arms, neck and legs, mostly.'

Nisha sagged against me and moaned a little. 'But he will be okay?'

The surgeon responded with a serious tone. 'I am optimistic but cautious. The next few days are going to be very critical and he is extremely susceptible to infection, which could be critical.'

'Can I see him?' she asked.

'He's in recovery right now, so it will be a little longer. I will warn you, though, he is going to be in an excruciating amount of pain and we will be keeping him heavily medicated for quite a while. He'll have to be in the hospital for at least a month as his burns heal and the skin starts to regenerate. When he is finally able to go home, his recovery will take several more months before he can return to any sort of work.'

Nisha nodded, tears streaming down her eyes. 'His café was destroyed so he has nothing to go back to anyway.'

The surgeon nodded sombrely. 'I heard and I'm very sorry. I've been to Kafe Kabir myself and it will be missed.'

Fighting through her tears, Nisha's chin lifted with determination. 'But he is alive and that is all that matters.'

'Yes,' he responded. 'That is all that matters.'

Those words echoed in my mind like wind chimes in the breeze when we were finally able to see Kabir. The human body is an amazing thing, that it can take so much trauma and keep going. But our dear friend was at the mercy of the medical world, as he was hooked up to more machinery than what runs my car.

Because of the risk of infection, Vivaan and I had to stay outside and watched tentatively through a window as Nisha, clad in a yellow medical suit and a mask, went in to see him. Before she walked through the doors, when she first saw him wrapped in bandages and obvious pain, I saw a look of sheer terror flash across her face before she wiped it away and replaced it with the soft, loving look that was pure Nisha.

Part of me felt like I was intruding on such a private moment, but I remembered her almost pleading request that we stay close for now. And, to be honest, after everything that happened, after the horrible fears that had dogged us through the day, I needed to lay eyes on our dear friend. Catching Vivaan's look of relief to see Kabir, even in this broken form, I knew he needed the same visual reassurance.

She sat near him, speaking slowly, soothingly. I watched her reach out a tentative hand, wanting to touch him, to ease his suffering. Then, she pulled back. Where could she touch him without causing more pain? Where was he not injured? Nisha turned sad eyes to us. I nodded, not knowing exactly what I was nodding for. Just reassurance, I guessed. We were there for her, Vivaan and me, and we would be by their sides as long as they wanted us there.

Soon, a nurse went to check on Kabir, ducking past us and then going into a small alcove to put a fresh hospital gown on. With fresh, germ-free clothing, the nurse checked Kabir's vital signs, making notes in his chart. She and Nisha exchanged some words, although, with the masks on, we had no idea what was being said.

Finally, the nurse reached out, squeezed Nisha's shoulder and left after shedding her disposable protection.

'How is he?' I asked the nurse.

'He is holding his own,' she said. 'He'll be very sleepy for several days... we are keeping him heavily sedated on purpose. His body needs to rest, and if he was awake, he would be in so much pain, he wouldn't be able to rest and heal.

'Has his wife eaten lately?' she continued.

I nodded. 'We were able to convince her to eat right before she went in to see Kabir.'

'Good,' the nurse said. 'She is going to need all the strength she has. Right now, she doesn't want to leave his side. And I can imagine I would be the same way if I was in that situation. She did tell me to let you know that you can go home if you want to, so you can get some rest.'

'We've already talked about it,' Vivaan said. 'I'm going to stay here, in case Kabir... Nisha... needs me. I'll take a nap in the waiting room.' He nodded toward the room a few steps away. 'The next time you go in, can you please let her know where I am?'

'And I'm going to go back to their house to take care of the baby and make more permanent arrangements. When I come back, I'll bring a change of clothes for Nisha. Is there anything I can bring back for Kabir?'

The nurse pursed her lips and considered. 'Does he have any favourite music? Anything that would give him a sense of connection to his old world?'

Vivaan and I exchanged a look. 'I'm sure I can find some of his favourite CDs to bring back. That is a great idea, thank you.'

'Of course,' she said and turned to leave.

I turned back to the window, waiting patiently until I caught Nisha's eye. With a few hand gestures, I let her know that Vivaan would be staying and that I would be going to her apartment to help Aashi with the baby.

In return, Nisha returned her own message of gratitude. I blew her a kiss and stepped away from the window. Giving Vivaan a tight hug, I gathered my belongings and left my three best friends behind me, torn between a need to stay and the driving desire to escape the sterile environment, even if just for a little while.

10

NISHA

It was silent, so silent as I listened to the sounds of the hospital at night. Kabir looked so small under all his bandages, his face rippling with pain, even as he slept.

I watched his chest rise and fall and watched the medicine dripping from the IV through the plastic tube into his arm. Every time he took a breath, I was relieved, but then immediately terrified. What if that was his last breath? What if there wasn't another one?

They say that right before you die, your life flashes in front of you, but watching Kabir struggling with his own survival made our life together flash in front of me, almost like someone was taking pictures and dropping them in front of me.

That very first time we met, when Kabir gave me the coffee and ice cream, I barely saw the man in front of me. I was so wrapped up in my own grief.

But even as the leaves are falling in autumn, you know that spring will come. It's a promise of the future, and Kabir was that for me. I loved him forever, but it wasn't until now that I realised how much. At this moment, I realised that the level of pain you feel for something proves how much it means to you. And oh, I was feeling pain.

Through his kindness and patience, his heart reached out to mine, and tentatively, I took his hand, starting on a beautiful journey of happiness and love together.

Your dreams don't disappear just because you lose your way and so slowly, I allowed myself to start dreaming again. Where I thought love was a lie, he showed me it was the truth.

The first time he asked me to marry him, I laughed bitterly. I didn't feel truly worthy of his love; I thought he was saving me. It took me a long time to realise that he wasn't trying to rescue me, that he actually wanted me.

He loved me, quietly, patiently. And oh, how I loved him too.

I recalled my pregnancy. Even as my body stretched around Jianna, to the point of utter discomfort, Kabir found a way to ease the pain, with his hands or his words.

What I wouldn't give to hear his hearty, deep laugh right now.

But here he was in front of me, wrapped in a blanket of never-ending pain. I wanted to pull him from the bed, plunge the IVs into my own arms and offer myself up to take the pain from him. If I could, I would have.

Tears dripped from my eyes, saturating the mask over my nose and mouth. What would I do if I lost him? How could I go on myself?

Early in the morning, I heard the door open and turned to see a nurse coming in. Silently, she checked his vital signs, noted the levels of medicine in the IV bags, and then turned to me.

'I think you need to take a little break,' she said quietly.

I shook my head. 'I need to stay here with Kabir.'

'I understand,' she said. 'Truly, I do. Your friend in the hall has been asking to see you though. Why don't I stay here while you go talk to him?'

I thought of Vivaan, our faithful friend, keeping vigil in the hallway too, and nodded. 'Just for a few minutes,' I agreed.

'Ask him to show you the courtyard,' she suggested. 'A little fresh air would do you good.'

I pressed my fingertips to the lips behind my mask, kissed them, and brushed the kiss onto Kabir's cheek. It felt warm and I frowned, wanting to stay. But I did want to speak with Vivaan, maybe convince him to go home for a little while.

I nodded to the nurse and told her I would be back in a few minutes, and then left the room, walking down the hall to the waiting area where Vivaan was sitting.

Although he was half asleep on the chair, he sprang to his feet when he saw me.

'Any change?' he said, rushing to hug me.

I shook my head. 'Nothing yet. I hate seeing him in so much pain, Vivaan,' I said, my voice wavering with more tears that wanted to break out.

'I know,' he said with a sigh. 'I wish there was something we could do. What I can do is take care of you for now. Do you want to get something to eat?'

I shook my head, nausea clawing at my stomach at the thought of food. 'I'm not hungry.'

'Let's go outside then,' he said. 'The nurse that just went into Kabir's room mentioned a courtyard.' He held out his hand. 'I'm not taking no for an answer,' he said firmly.

I allowed myself to be tugged down the hall and we stepped into a beautiful, peaceful area draped with lush green plants. There was a small fountain and even though it was hot, the shade of the trees and the moving water seemed to keep away the stolid heat.

We sat on a smooth stone bench for a good half hour. I was lost in my thoughts of Kabir, but Vivaan pressed on with a one-sided conversation.

Suddenly, the peace I felt was ripped away from me. 'I need to go back in,' I said, standing up quickly. 'Something's wrong.'

To his credit, Vivaan didn't try to placate me but stepped ahead of me to open the door.

I retraced my steps back to Kabir's room, but terror froze my feet when we turned a corner and I saw the activity of people rushing in and out of his room. I looked at Vivaan, and his eyes were wide with fright.

'Kabir!' I cried and started to run the rest of the way.

A nurse saw me approaching and reached out to stop me. 'We need you to stay outside for now.'

'No,' I cried. I felt Vivaan's arms circling around me. I pushed at him, trying to get to Kabir. 'I need to go to Kabir!'

'He has a high temperature,' the nurse explained quickly. 'He started to seize. Please, we need space to work on him right now.'

Vivaan pulled me aside, out of the way of the rushing medical staff. 'Give them room, Nisha. They need to focus all their efforts on Kabir.'

My legs gave out from under me and I slid to the cold floor. Vivaan eased me down and then knelt beside me, glancing around to make sure we were out of the way.

'Kabir,' I heard myself moan. 'What if I lose Kabir?'

Tears streamed down my face and I wrapped my arms around myself and started rocking slowly. Back and forth, like I was rocking Jianna. With his eyes on the medical staff, he reached out and took my hand.

'Vivaan,' I choked out, 'what is happening?'

He shook his head. 'I don't know,' he said. 'I'll try to find out.'

'No!' I said. 'Please, don't leave me.'

'Okay,' he said and settled into a sitting position beside me. I clung to his hand, squeezing tightly. My hand hurt with the effort, but the pain felt good. It anchored me to the hallway.

Finally, a doctor left Kabir's room, still barking out orders to the nurse. He glanced our way and started to walk over. I scrambled to my feet, Vivaan doing the same.

I wanted to ask what happened, but the words didn't come. What if Kabir had died? *No!* I shook my head violently, tears clinging to my cheeks. My legs shook and threatened to buckle again, but Vivaan held me up this time.

The doctor took a deep breath and I could see the weariness in his eyes. 'Kabir has stabilised again, but he has a very high fever. He started to go into a seizure.'

The few bits of food in my stomach churned and threatened to erupt. I pushed my hand against my mouth and started to breathe hard. I made a whining sound, horrible even to my own ears. How could I have left him? He was okay when I left, I should have stayed! I should never have gone to that stupid courtyard. I should...

'Fortunately,' the doctor said, breaking into my thoughts, 'the nurse was right there so he was in good hands.'

'So the fever caused a seizure?' I whispered.

'It can happen when a fever is very high,' he responded. 'I have to warn you, although the seizure is over, and we are taking steps to bring his temperature down, the situation just got even more critical. A fever often indicates an infection, which can...'

His words trailed off, but I knew what that meant: Kabir could die.

He might die, and I could still lose him...

I fell against Vivaan.

'He's strong though,' the doctor continued. 'And he has a lot to fight for. I heard you have a young daughter.'

I nodded, but couldn't speak. My throat burned, and I started to shake.

Our life was so good. How could that just be yanked away from us so abruptly?

'We added another medication to combat any infection and we will be watching him closely. If you will excuse me, I'm going to go check on him.'

I nodded dumbly and watched him go back into Kabir's room.

Vivaan tugged on my arm. 'Let's go sit in the waiting room so we'll be out of the way here,' he suggested. He told the nurses where to find us and led me to the waiting room where he had been sleeping.

'How?' I whispered once I was sitting down. 'How could all of our dreams just disappear like that?'

Vivaan shook his head. 'They haven't disappeared, Nisha,' he said with urgency in his voice. 'You have to hold on to that.'

'My heart is breaking,' I cried. 'I can't see any dreams right now. I just see us losing them.'

'Like what?' he asked gently.

'Kabir! My family. Oh God, Vivaan…. How can I go on if I lose him?' I buried my face in my hands and started sobbing. 'I just can't…'

I felt Vivaan slide to his knees in front of me and pulled my hands away, so I was forced to look at him. 'You have to hold on to hope, Nisha! As the rains pour down, sometimes it seems like you'll never see the sun again, but it still comes.'

'Even now?'

'Even now. There is one part of the night that is the coldest and the darkest: before dawn breaks. Just when we might give up on seeing the light again, the sun breaks over the horizon. Kabir will make it. He has to.'

11
FATE

You must despise me right now, don't you? Kabir and Nisha had a cosy little life with their cosy little family. Everything was going so good for them.

I allowed that... for a time. But this is how I work. Things can't be all good, all the time, can they?

I'm sure you're all optimistic and are thinking that they have to go through struggles to appreciate the good times, right?

Dreams yield hope. Without those dreams, you have nothing. You may try to avoid your destiny, but it is waiting for you, no matter the path you take. It will find you.

I don't really care if they are struggling. I don't make them struggle to enjoy the better times. I make them struggle because they deserve it.

Nobody should be happy all the time. If people tell you that they're happy all the time, they're lying.

I just force people to see the truth in life. I bring it front and centre and plop it right into their laps.

Call it Karma. Call *me* Karma.

Nobody is perfect, and I make them pay for those imperfections. I make them struggle and writhe through life. Why? Because it's fun.

Have you ever watched a cat play with a mouse? It doesn't always kill the mouse right away... it'll catch it, and let it go. Let it think that it has a chance at life. And just as it starts to scurry away, the cat pounces once again. This can go on and on until the mouse finally dies.

Hopefully, the cat's owner doesn't step on it in the morning.

But you know, listening to a screaming cat owner can be fun in itself. Kind of a bonus, in my humble opinion.

I tricked you, didn't I? I'm not humble. I am power. Just like that cat, I can toy with your emotions. I can make promises, and whisk them away just as easily.

Do yourself a favour and make sure you wear shoes … and tread lightly around me.

12

KABIR

I don't remember ever being excited and filled with dread at the same time. After one very long month in the hospital, it was time for me to go home.

I looked out the window at the same view that had kept me company for so many weeks. Every morning, I woke to the same building tops, and every night, I watched them dissolve into the darkness, to be replaced by the lights from inside those buildings.

Some days, I liked the consistency; it was something I could focus on when I was trying to ignore the constant nag of pain.

I hurt all the time. It was always there, reminding me of that horrible day. Some moments, the medication could keep it more manageable, but other times, especially before my next dose of painkiller was due, the pain took over more and more of my mind, rising like a great, ugly, fire-breathing beast.

No matter my level of pain, it always came as a sharp, white dagger whenever the doctors came and poked at me. I knew they had to check on me and check my progress. But even something as light as a stray hair on my new skin was agony, forget when the doctors prodded, or the nurses changed my bandages.

I learned this in the hospital: the winds will blow and howl around you. The rains will threaten and terrify. You will reach a point when you don't know if you can survive, but know this: the winds will blow themselves out, the clouds will empty of the rain. Gradually, the storm ends, so slowly that you won't even notice at first. You will emerge changed, not altered by the elements but by your own will to survive.

Gradually, the intensity of my pain diminished. It was still there, still a great beast in the room, ready to bite at me when I least expected it. But it was getting better.

And now, I was going home.

So, why was I dreading that change that I so desperately desired at the same time?

I knew I would be happy to be home, yes. To be in my own bed, to sit in my favourite chair that Nisha said was too ugly to keep. To smell the scents of her cooking, instead of this plastic antiseptic smell that I was sure was going to cling to me like an aura for years to come. To hear my precious Jianna giggling, or even arguing stubbornly that she wanted another biscuit or didn't want a bath... I didn't care. I just wanted to be a part of every phase of her toddlerhood.

And the dread? Sadly, the list was much longer. Even just going home scared me to death. That hot, pressing sun outside the climate control of the hospital. My baby skin was so sensitive now, even a degree or two marked the difference between comfort and agony. While I was at the hospital, Nisha, Vivaan, and Meera encouraged me to go outside and sit in the lush green hospital courtyard, but I was careful to sit in the shade. It was safe, predictable. Sure, a small breeze might blow the branches above me, but if that happened, I could scamper inside.

Now, what if the car I was to go home in turned a corner and suddenly, my burns were exposed to blistering sunlight?

And when I got home, how could I protect myself from that scampering, energetic toddler? I used to love it when Jianna would jump in my lap. What if she did that when I wasn't expecting it? I didn't want to keep my little girl away from me, but I had to protect myself from getting hurt. She would be terrified if I reacted to the pain and cried out.

Maybe I wasn't ready. Maybe I needed to stay in the hospital for another week. Even a day or two, I didn't care. I would be healed that much more. I sat heavily on the chair in my room, turning my back to the window. If I was going to stay here longer, those buildings would drive me crazy.

The hospital bill beside me wasn't giving me any strength. I don't think I was supposed to see it yet, but in these last few days in the hospital, I wandered the halls, gaining some endurance, pushing my smoke-damaged lungs to heal faster. One day, I entered the billing office and requested a copy of my bill. I knew someone was keeping track of it, and I was the patient, after all. I suspected that Nisha had a copy of the mounting costs, but she kept it from me. Until that moment.

So sitting beside me on the hospital bed I was expected to abandon today was the monetary value of my care. My surgeries, the medicines, the rounds from each doctor and nurse, the cost of living in my semi-private room. What happened in a few moments at Kafe Kabir that day—really, the time it took to take and fill an order for the most basic cup of coffee—came with a price tag of ten lakh rupees.

Ten lakhs. How could so much damage be done in such a short amount of time?

And... how could we possibly pay this bill?

Vivaan walked into my hospital room, a huge grin on his face. 'Ready to go home?' he said, beaming and rubbing his hands together in heavy expectation.

I quickly tucked away my reservations but my brave, tight-lipped smile must have given me away. Nisha always said my smile was like a television screen, projecting my feelings honestly and clearly, no matter how much I may try to hide them.

Vivaan's eyebrow cocked in question and he sat down on the hospital bed in front of me. His feet swung helplessly before he reached for the controls and lowered the bed. Then, with his shoes planted firmly on the hospital tile, he rested his elbows on his knees and leaned forward. 'Talk to me, Kabir,' he ordered.

I snorted a little dismissively and looked away from his piercing, bright glance. 'Talk to you about what?'

'What is bothering you? I know something is,' he responded. 'After being here for so many weeks, I was thinking you'd be running out that door.'

There was no sense in lying to my good friend. After all, he and Meera had us shown their faithfulness and dedication this month. They didn't hesitate to set their own lives aside to help both me and Nisha. Meera was an endless source of strength for Nisha, helping her with Jianna at the apartment so Nisha could be by my side, giving her support every moment when my own confidence in my healing would fail.

I knew, even though Nisha never confessed any weak moments, that Meera was there, holding her up when she faltered as well. So, when Nisha was with me, she was a ball of positive energy.

And Vivaan. I didn't know if he and Nisha had worked out a schedule between them, but if she wasn't with me, he was. I was never alone. If I was sleeping, I would wake to see Vivaan quietly sitting in a chair, reading a book. And if I was awake, he was there. The doctors and nurses were fantastic, but he had this uncanny way of seeing what I needed and wordlessly making it happen.

It was Vivaan who broke the news to me that Kafe Kabir had been destroyed. I didn't know for sure what had happened to my business and when I'd ask Nisha, she would smile, pat my bed and declare that we'd work everything else out.

'Nisha, please.' I usually left her alone about the café because when I pushed, she'd get this pained twitch like lemon juice had just squirted her in the eye. I guess I knew the truth because I didn't push the issue. I had already brought so much discomfort to our family with my injuries. But one day, I just couldn't stand it and I begged her for the truth. 'I need to know. What happened to the cafe? Was it destroyed? Damaged? What? Tell me.'

I could see the denial was already forming on her lips when she started to break down, tears rising in her eyes. My loving, strong wife closed those beautiful lids, somehow pushed the tears away and when they lifted again, only a little dampness clung to her long lashes.

'It will be fine,' she declared firmly.

I left it alone but repeated the questions when Vivaan came in, pretending to smuggle a serving of malai kofta from one of my favourite restaurants. Nisha was going home to shower and have dinner with Jianna, so I knew I had a couple hours with Vivaan. I would pry the truth out of him, one way or another.

And my good friend told me everything. The café was destroyed, and nothing had been salvaged. Not even a coffee bean. The pictures I had so painstakingly selected to enhance the ambience, the bright red and white striped cushions on the sofas in the corner. Nothing left. All of it was gone.

I didn't react much when he told me the truth that day; in fact, I really knew. I just needed the words spoken to seal the envelope on my dreams.

Now, though, with all my emotions on the surface, barely protected by this thin layer of new skin that both protected and marred my body, I let the truth rise up. I heard that tsunamis sucked the water down the ocean sands, gathering strength before they attacked a wall of merciless, killing water. My tears did the same, trickling one at a time down my cheeks before a torrent was unleashed, pushing past my eyes so fast it was almost like the organs had disappeared, letting the tears erupt with no obstacles.

I heard, rather than saw, Vivaan push off the bed and kneel on the floor beside me. I felt his strong hands wrap around mine, carefully putting his reassuring pressure on my undamaged skin, rather than my healing areas.

I don't know how long my friend knelt on the floor before me, letting me shed the bitter, scared, frustrated tears that I had kept so carefully filtered from my 'normal' life, the one that didn't allow random emotions.

As my tears started to abate, he slid onto the large chair beside me and took my broken form into his large embrace. Embarrassed even then by my weakness, I turned my head to his presence, seeking the normalcy my best friend offered.

Then, I shook my head, suddenly embarrassed, and sat up quickly, using the unbroken parts of my hands to push away the rest of the tears.

'Vivaan,' I started, mortified. 'I didn't... I mean...'

I was not a man who let sentences settle unfinished. I was raised to be strong, to say what I felt, unapologetically. But here I was, a crumpled pile of wilted crepe paper made up of tear-stained nothingness. I despised the feeling.

'I am sorry,' I said.

'Don't be. Crying yields a force within yourself that will allow you to do many things—healing, forgiving, or sustaining. Allow those tears sometimes, and one day you won't need them anymore because you will have healed.'

'Healing.' I scoffed at that word.

'Kabir,' Vivaan responded helplessly. 'Tell me what is going on.'

I sniffled. 'I'm not sure I can, to be perfectly honest.'

'Try,' he said urgently. 'Kabir, please. We all thought you'd be happy to go home. What has changed?'

I hung my head, letting the weight of my problems pull it down for a few moments. 'It's... everything. Vivaan,' I asked, almost pleading, 'how did things change so fast? I know I've had a month to come to terms with everything but truly, how did it happen? One minute, I was on the top of the world... of course, to me at the time, it was just another normal day. But it was good; it was the constant I knew.'

I took in Vivaan's face, twisting with his own empathetic pain.

'And then,' I continued, 'it all changed in the blink of an eye. Now here I am, some hideous version of the Kabir I was.' As he would, I knew Vivaan was catching his breath to argue, the faithful companion he was.

I wouldn't let him speak though. 'Don't,' I commanded.

His breath let out, but he said nothing.

I kept going. 'People used to come to Kafe Kabir simply because of what we offered.'

'And that was?' Vivaan whispered.

'Consistency, for starters,' I said. 'They came for the same darn cup of coffee every day. One cream? Two sugars? Didn't matter. When they left with their coffee, they could trust that it tasted the same that it did yesterday, and two weeks ago. And would taste in the next month or even year.

'But it was more than that. We were a normal group of people, so normal that we were really background music. Friendly music, yes, but only secondary because we were so ... normal.

'Look at me,' I commanded and Vivaan's eyes caught mine. 'NO!' I insisted. 'Look at my arms, my hands, my neck. What do you see?'

I knew he was uncomfortable, even though he barely squirmed under the discomfort. Instead, his eyes raked over my burned skin, his gaze so intense, it was almost physical and I winced a little. My voice lowered, but I persisted. 'What do you see, Vivaan?'

His eyes lifted to mine once more. 'I see you.'

'You see a tarnished me,' I argued.

'No, Kabir,' he insisted. 'I see you. Changed a bit, yes. But these scars'—he waved his hand over the whitish tissue—'and this'—hovering over my pink, tight, new skin—'this is all part of Kabir. Scars may change the appearance of the skin, but they are the way the body heals, and when the scar is formed, it adds a layer of strength that didn't exist before.'

'You say that so easily,' I responded darkly.

'Healing will be the most difficult thing you ever do. But it's also the most important.'

I wanted to believe his simple words, but I simply couldn't. 'Don't you see, Vivaan? My differences, these scars, these are all signposts screaming 'I'm different!' I don't want people to be uncomfortable around me.'

'You are still you, Kabir. We hurt for a reason. Pain tells us there is a problem. If we don't feel it, we can't fix it. Do you understand?'

'No. It has changed. Kafe Kabir was a success because it was unchanging. Now, everything has changed. There isn't even...' I choked on my own emotions once more before clearing my throat again. 'There isn't even a Kafe Kabir. It's ... gone,' I ended in a whisper of agony.

'We'll rebuild,' he argued.

'I can't start over,' I said helplessly. 'Look at this.' I handed him the hospital bill and let his eyes take in all the numbers. 'Ten lakhs,' I said. 'I don't have this kind of money! Everything I had, all our savings for my family and our new café, has gone in my treatment. I can't pay this AND rebuild!'

Vivaan took his time reading the tallied charges before he swept the bill aside and stood up angrily. 'You can't think of this now,' he said.

'How?' I cried. 'How can I ignore this?'

Once again, Vivaan sat at the foot of the hospital bed,

frowning at me. 'Do. Not. Give. This. Power.' I sat back at my friend's ferociously determined words.

'I have to,' I said. 'It's reality.'

'No!' he barked. 'Reality is this: You were hurt. You could have DIED, Kabir! After your accident, Nisha, Meera, and I watched you fight for every next breath. At first, every few moments. Then, you fought for the next minute, then the next hour, then the next day. You've been through nothing short of hell. But it's not over.'

Wow, so much for an optimistic pep talk, I thought dryly.

'I'm tired of fighting,' I argued.

'You are tired, but you can't be tired of fighting, Kabir. The pain goes away. Giving up does not. Giving up remains with you forever, a thorn in your shoe. You are still healing. You need to keep healing, and it isn't going to happen if you're worried about bills and rebuilding, and everything else.'

'And what do you suggest?' I asked bitterly.

'Heal.'

I expected more but he left it at that one word. It wasn't enough for me.

'That's it. Heal.'

'Yes, Kabir,' he said. 'Put all your energy into rebuilding that skin, and fixing those scars. Find the new Kabir, the one who was hurt but the one who moved beyond that damage. But it's more than just on the outside. You need to heal on the inside, too.'

'How do you mean?'

'When you heal, you don't just force the hurt aside. Pain is actually a welcome feeling because it means that you have not closed yourself off to life. You need to learn how to embrace it as your companion, for a little while. Allow it to coexist with you for the time being; don't use it to mark when your life ended, but where it began again. If

I could, my friend, I would take away this pain. But even if I held my arms out as wide as possible, I could never capture all the hurt.'

I laughed bitterly. 'Don't take this the wrong way, but that is easy for you to say.'

His eyebrows raised. 'I am your friend, Kabir. Don't you realise how much I would take on if I could? Friends stand by you no matter what. If you are hurting, they share your shadows, and when you celebrate, they are there to share the sunshine. I'm there with you in the darkness right now, as much as I want to tug you back into the light.'

As he said that, I felt his words wash over me, and for a moment, the pain was simply gone.

'What about Kafe Kabir?' I asked.

'We'll figure it out when the time is right,' he said reassuringly. 'I was there for you in the beginning, right?'

I smiled tightly. 'Yes,' I admitted. 'I couldn't have started my business without your investment. And your confidence in me.'

'That confidence is still there, my friend,' Vivaan said, leaning forward and squeezing my arm. 'And the investment will be there again. Life can hand us garbage, but we need to use it to fertilise our hopes and dreams once more. We will be together every step of the way. Yes, there is still pain but you don't need to let yourself get hurt.'

I said nothing. What could I say? I couldn't keep taking from the man. But he seemed to read my thoughts and spoke again. 'Anytime now, investors will commit to my project and I can start my own business. It'll grow exponentially,' he said confidently, 'and then I'll have the money to put back into helping you rebuild your business.'

'I can't—'

'When you are fully healed,' he said, interrupting me, 'we will rebuild. You have to keep pushing ahead, even when things seem hopeless. You'll find when you look back that you had a strength you never knew was in you before.'

I looked at him, seeing his determination, but also seeing admiration in his face. A man only truly knows his worth when he sees himself in another person's eyes.

My throat was tight once more, dammed up by the emotions of his pledge. All I could do was purse my lips and nod. 'Okay,' I whispered.

Vivaan smiled. 'Ready to go now?' he asked, and I nodded. 'Let me go and see what is keeping the discharge nurse. They should be bringing your final forms any minute!'

He swept out of the room with an air of determination. Our conversation had helped alleviate a lot of my fears, but my anger was still there.

'Damn you, Fate,' I spat. 'You stole my livelihood from me. You could have let me continue my happy life, but no! You thought it would be fun to toy with my life! I swear this to you, you will not win.'

13

VIVAAN

'Okay, thank you for letting me know,' I said, the sense of defeat making my words thick and hard to vocalise.

I hung up the phone and started pacing. That was the third potential investor that had rejected my proposal for Musafir. How could this be happening? They seemed to like the idea when I first met them but now it seemed like a different story.

I sat down at the table in front of me and turned on my laptop. I clicked on the file that listed potential investor information. Sadly, I highlighted the name of the gentleman I just spoken to with two alphabets: 'NO'.

Discouraged, I looked at the other names, trying to visualize each one and their expressions when I had met them.

One name caught my attention: Daksh Chandran. I recalled he seemed very interested in the presentation, his eyes lighting up as I mentioned various places where I could take groups. Picking up my phone once again, I called Mr Chandran.

He answered the phone cheerfully and I introduced myself.

'Ah, Vivaan,' he said, his voice a little more guarded. 'I was planning to call you soon. I'm sure you are wondering what my decision is on investing in your little company.'

Uh oh, 'your little company' doesn't sound very promising, I thought to myself. I tried to ignore the thought and responded to his comment. 'Yes, sir,' I said respectfully. 'Are there any other questions that you have for me that will help you make your final decision on investing in my startup?'

I heard him sigh at the other end of the phone and my hand clenched nervously. 'Let me ask you one question. You said before you started exploring parts of India, you traveled to different areas of the world.'

'That's right, I did.'

'Why?' he asked bluntly.

'It is as I mentioned in my presentation, I didn't realise the true beauty that was right in our backyard. The history, the different regions. I thought I wanted more; I thought I needed to leave our country to learn about the world.'

'Ah, yes,' he said.

I realised he was leading me down the wrong path, one that would end up rejecting my tour company, and was quick to explain. 'But, I also said that was wrong; that the riches of India had claimed my heart. It is these areas that I want to show to people.'

'Would that younger Vivaan have listened to someone about the beauties of India?'

I shook my head sadly. I wanted to lie to him, to tell him that if someone had sold the idea of staying in our country to me at that age, I would have stayed. But I remembered my desire to escape the borders of our country. 'I would listen to me now,' was all I could say.

'But before,' he pressed on.

Now it was my turn to sigh. I closed my eyes, praying for a fleck of inspiration as I spoke to this man, but the sense of defeat was too much. I couldn't push through it to find those reasons to stay.

Mr Chandran continued. 'I think it's a good idea, Vivaan. I truly do.'

I started to brighten up a little and stood from my chair excitedly. 'So you will be willing to invest in Musafir? That's terrific!'

'You misunderstand me,' he said, and my heart sank once

more. 'I, personally, like the idea. But I am one person, I am an old man. The demographic you speak of targeting is nowhere near my age,' he said, chuckling a little. 'I'm sorry, Vivaan. I did some research of my own and the younger generations are determined to leave India.'

'So we give them a reason to stay!' I was growing desperate.

'Making the assumption that this demographic will have such an abrupt change of heart is a dangerous gamble,' he said sadly. 'I thought about this long and hard, and my answer is no. I cannot risk my finances in an investment such as this. Perhaps later, when you are established and are ready to expand, I may reconsider. But for now... people want to travel abroad, and not India.'

I couldn't change his mind, and to push any harder would just make me look like a fool. And put off any potential investment opportunities in the future. I walked to the window and looked out, beyond the building tops. My beautiful, beloved India, these jungles, temples, and castles, they were just waiting for people to appreciate them. If people could just look beyond the dusty cities, they would realise how foolish they were to hop on a plane and escape to other countries.

'Thank you for your time, sir,' I said. 'I appreciate your honesty and am grateful that you took the time to speak with me.'

'I hope I'm wrong,' Mr Chandran said.

I laughed, aware that there was a sadness in the sound. 'I too hope you are.'

Disconnecting the call, I trudged back to my laptop and sadly highlighted his name, writing 'No' beside it.

Over the next several days, I reached out to everyone on my list and got the same response from each one; some regretful like Daksh Chandran, others practically calling my idea crazy. 'Nobody wants to spend money to see India,' one man said in a condescending tone. 'When they spend money travelling, they want their money to take them to other places, not their backyard! Your dream is just that: a dream. A rather insane one, if you ask me.'

I wanted to flee, to lose myself, and bury my frustration. With an almost desperate need, I packed my travel bag and prepared for another trip. My destination? The caves in Tabo, I decided. I could hide away in the darkness, and wait for the sting of rejection to heal itself.

I picked up my bag, stalking to the door. Then, sighing, I dropped it on to the colourful rug near the front door. I couldn't run now, not while Kabir still needed me. He was home and while he was healing physically, he was still hurting emotionally. No, I needed to stay and lean on my friends, the way I had encouraged them to lean on me since that horrible fire.

I called Meera and asked her to meet me at Kabir and Nisha's apartment. Then, I called and spoke with Nisha, suggesting that I get some takeout food from one of Kabir's favourite restaurants and come over. 'I've asked Meera to meet me at your place, too. I would like to talk to the three of you.'

'Of course,' Nisha responded. 'I haven't started preparing dinner yet, so this will be a welcome break.'

I knew Nisha was picking up on my tense aura, but she wasn't going to comment on it over the phone. I appreciated her sensitivity. She was an extremely wise woman.

'I'll see you soon,' I said and hung up.

An hour later, we gathered at the table. Even Kabir, who often took his meals where he could be comfortable in the living room, insisted on coming to the table to eat. I wondered if Nisha had clued him into the serious tone of my voice when I spoke to her.

I didn't have long to wonder. We had barely started eating when Kabir looked at me pointedly. 'Something is wrong,' he said bluntly.

I sighed and pushed the plate away from me. I had no appetite anyway, so there was no sense putting off what I had to tell them.

'The investors turned down Musafir,' I started, and looked around the table at my dear friends, watching the emotions playing over their faces, like ripples in a lake. There was shock and sadness. But then I saw determination.

'Maybe you can start on a smaller scale,' Kabir suggested. 'Create a small tour group, keep your own payment down, maybe as an introductory rate.'

Nisha nodded. 'Small steps,' she said. 'Create a following with a small number of people. Capture their experiences, and use them in your marketing plan.'

'Test your success,' Kabir continued. 'We all know it's going to be a success; you just need to prove it.'

'Can you go back to your investors, once you're established?' Meera asked.

I thought about it, mentally going through the list. I wouldn't crawl back to the people who outright laughed at me, but there were a handful of others, like Mr Chandran, who expressed true regret in having to turn down the investment opportunity. If I could come back with a successful pilot programme, perhaps they would be more willing to listen a second time.

'I think it's a good idea,' I agreed. 'There are some that would be keen to invest if I could prove the success. I didn't really think to start small, but it's a good idea, Kabir.'

The four of us spoke at length about how to best revamp the plan I had to scale it down to a more local group for now. There were plenty of areas that I could take people at a reasonable rate as the test groups. As we spoke, I began to get extremely excited and even started eating again. The food was getting cold, but I didn't care.

'Where will you get your finances though?' Nisha asked, frowning with her concern.

'I have about five lakh rupees saved from my share of the profits from Kafe Kabir,' I said, wincing as I said the name. Perhaps I shouldn't have mentioned the name of Kabir's beloved coffee shop. But it was important because I had another subject to bring up.

Nisha brightened when she heard the figure. It was a modest sum, but she had a good head for figures and as a young mother, she thrived in opportunities to make something out of nothing.

'I did have another thought I wanted to speak to you three about, though,' I started again, looking directly at Kabir. This next question was for everyone, but it probably concerned him the most.

'Yes?' Kabir said. He sat back, and I could tell he was starting to get uncomfortable from sitting at the table for so long. I suggested we take the conversation into the living room, where we could all sit comfortably.

Nisha and Meera took care of the dishes, and I slowly walked Kabir into the living room, carefully helping him to settle in his most comfortable chair. It was a drawn-out process and by the time we were ready to resume the conversation, Nisha and Meera rejoined us, after checking on Jianna, who was sleeping peacefully in her cot.

I didn't really know where to start, even though I was trying to collect my thoughts in the few minutes since we had left the table.

They waited patiently for me to find my starting point, although I could tell on all their faces that they were curious to hear what I had to say.

'I have five lakh rupees,' I started again. 'But I'm not sure if it is the best idea to use that to start Musafir.'

Meera gasped. 'Why? Vivaan, this is your dream!'

'But there are other dreams and there is another story that needs to continue.' I looked at Kabir and took a deep breath. 'Maybe we should use the money to rebuild Kafe Kabir instead.'

Kabir let out a little cry. 'Oh Vivaan, no.'

'No?' I repeated, surprised. Perhaps I had been reading him wrong all these weeks. Maybe he spoke about rebuilding, but didn't really want to return to the café life.

He quickly dispelled that thought, leaning forward urgently in his chair. 'Kafe Kabir will be rebuilt, but it can wait,' he said, looking at Nisha, who nodded her agreement. 'I think,' he continued, 'that the most urgent need is to start Musafir.'

'But...'

'It's final,' Kabir said firmly.

I smiled, feeling a tingle of pleasure run through down my arms. These friends, they meant so much to me. But to hear Kabir's determination in supporting my company, and to see Nisha and Meera's glistening eyes as they emphatically agreed... it was overwhelming.

I thought fleetingly at my urgency only a few hours ago, to flee to some dark caves, and I felt foolish. This was what I needed. Not some cold cave somewhere, that wouldn't fix me. I needed the warm, bright encouragement of these three people. When is a friendship formed? I wondered fleetingly. Just like falling in love, there is never an actual starting point; it just is, filling your heart with minute moments.

I saw an amazing sight. It was that look you share with a friend that shows you that they truly understand you. They all had that same strong, steady gaze.

I wanted to say something but some emotions cannot be put into words. If you try, you take away their power. I knew this though. Friends more valuable than gold. They know us in a way that we don't even know ourselves, laughing during our celebrations and crying in our disappointments.

I'm not much for crying, but I could feel the tears welling up in my eyes. 'Thank you,' I whispered, unable to speak any louder. 'I can't tell you how much I appreciate each and every one of you.' I realised then how much people need people. Nobody can know anything or do anything all by themselves. If you want to truly succeed, you need the support of many.

They understood what I needed like daytime understands the night.

'When the time is right,' Meera suggested, 'we can use some of the profits from Musafir to rebuild Kafe Kabir.'

I agreed. 'That is a very good idea.'

'Now it's my turn to say something,' Meera continued. Everyone turned to her and for the first time this evening, I noticed a satisfied smile playing around her lips. 'I've been in negotiations with my publishers, as you know. We are almost ready to close the deal.'

'That is terrific,' Nisha breathed. 'Judging from the look on your face, the negotiations are going very well!'

Meera nodded happily. 'Better than I could have ever dreamed!'

'Do you have a figure yet?'

She shook her head. 'We haven't agreed on a final price yet, but I can tell you that it is already much greater than my other books.'

'That is fantastic!' I said, leaning over and wrapping my arms around her. 'I am not surprised, though. You are a very talented woman and, of course, your publishers want to keep you happy.'

'As long as things continue to go well—and I have every confidence that they will—I should be getting the advance within a month or two. We can use that money to help boost Musafir *and* rebuild Kafe Kabir!'

I stood up quickly and pulled Meera to her feet. 'Vivaan!' she cried happily. I wrapped my arms around her and picked her up, spinning her around as she laughed. I closed my eyes and buried my face in her hair.

Before the night was over, we agreed that I would move forward as soon as possible with my limited funds to start organising my startup, and then Meera—now the co-owner of Musafir—would contribute part of her advance when it was time to launch the company.

After so many rough weeks, I was starting to believe that fate was starting to smile at us once more.

14

VIVAAN

One month later

Sitting in Kabir and Nisha's living room a month ago, I knew good things were just beginning. After that night, I threw myself into launching my tour company.

Everyone was so incredibly supportive, especially Kabir, who had a scary setback a few weeks ago when an infection took root in his body. One minute, he was fine; the next, Nisha called me, frantic, because his fever had spiked once again.

Fortunately, a night in the hospital and some strong antibiotics took care of the infection, but they set him back a few steps. In typical Kabir fashion, though, he shifted his energy into helping me with some of the details only an experienced small business owner would think about. His insights were priceless and each day we came closer to the first tour, excitement surrounded all of us like an unexpectedly warm day after a series of chilly weeks.

'Tell me a little more about yourself,' I said to the man sitting in front of me. He was the tenth interviewee that day and what felt like the hundredth that week. When she could, Meera sat in on the interviews with me, but I suggested she stay home today, knowing that she was having trouble with the pace of her writing. I saw it in each random frown when she was lost in her thoughts.

The older man sat back in his chair and took a deep breath. 'I used to be a truck driver many moons ago,' he started. 'It was a good job but there was a lot of pressure to get loads in on time, to make sure the trucks were full but never too full. It wore me down.'

I wrinkled my nose in sympathy. 'I can imagine,' I said.

'But I love to drive, and I'm very comfortable driving buses. I'm pretty sure I was born with a steering wheel in my hands! I love seeing new places so when I saw this ad, I thought it was the perfect solution for me. After all, since I retired, I'm driving my beloved wife crazy. I think it's either get a job or get a divorce,' he said, with a twinkle in his eye.

I laughed and knew he would be the perfect addition to the staff members I already hired, thanks to the savings Meera had invested.

My staff would help organise the next tour, so I could focus my energies on taking care of my customers when the first tour was going on. I was amazed at how many people had already signed up for more tours. With Meera's social media connections, I had even been contacted by a small, but very successful business that wanted to use Musafir's services to take their top staff members on a business retreat of sorts.

Every now and then, I'd think about the investors that turned me down. I thought everything was falling apart but it wasn't. I realised that our path may change and events may settle in like obstacles, but if we continue to move forward, we will be ultimately successful.

After the interview was over, I walked him to the door. Turning around to look at the office, I felt myself nod approvingly at how much we had accomplished in such a short time. The hard work had been so worth it to get to this point.

Those dark days when I listened to the investor after investor turn me down, I felt like such a failure. But failure is not the end—it's the beginning of a new chance to make your life even better. We cannot avoid the fate that is ours, but we can choose to walk that path with a positive step.

As the pieces came together with Musafir, things didn't always happen smoothly. But those challenges strengthened my resolve to continue.

There are wins in our lives every day. They might be big, like getting a new job, or they might be as small as getting out of bed in the morning when we really want to pull the blankets over our head. No matter the size, these successes should be embraced. Right now, they came in small steps, but steps closer to opening the business.

We decided that the first tour should be to Rajasthan because it was relatively close but far enough to be a great adventure for our clients. I couldn't wait to see the look on their faces when visiting the Ranakpur Jain Temple, seeing for themselves the 1,444 intricate carved columns.

We would also be visiting Kumbalgarh, also known as India's Great Wall, the Meera Temple and Chittorgarh Fort.

I rented a tour bus to take our twenty-eight clients. This would help keep costs low, and I could take the time over the fifteen-hour trip to Udaipur to clarify the rules and fill our clients in on the people and places where we would be visiting. After all, even though we were compensating people for opening up their homes to our guests, we wanted to ensure that they had a good experience as well.

It would also give me time to brainstorm about other trips. The next one, I hoped, would be even better than this first one, because Meera would be with me. For this trip, we had decided that she would stay behind in Pune. That way, she could help Nisha with the baby and help Kabir, who was still weak after his most recent infection.

Nisha and I both made a list of friends who lived in or near Chittorgarh, Udaipur, and other cities along the route, and we were quickly able to convince them to host the tour group while we were in these areas. Those who were unable to accommodate such a large group were more than happy to provide my staff with a list of popular local restaurants and other events that might otherwise not capture the attention of larger tour groups.

Soon enough, all was set. I bid goodbye to Nisha and Kabir, who gave me one last surprise. Without my knowledge, Kabir had reached out to one of his former employees to go to my apartment. Meera gave the woman, Yamini, the spare key that she had for my apartment. When we arrived there, I was delighted to find a beautiful, intimate dinner had been prepared for us.

Candles were lit on the table, and two places were set for us.

I couldn't believe it. I was so touched by our friends' thoughtfulness. I quickly called Kabir before sitting down. 'Thank you for this, Kabir!' I said as soon as he picked up the phone.

It was good to hear him laugh uncontrollably for the first time in a long time. 'You are welcome, Vivaan! You and Meera have been so good to us, so we wanted you to have one last quiet evening with Meera before you leave.'

I shook my head, overwhelmed. 'This is perfect ...' I started before Kabir interrupted me.

'Stop talking and go enjoy your evening!'

I laughed. 'Yes sir,' I said in mock seriousness. 'Thank you aga—' But I never had a chance to finish the sentence because Kabir hung up on me.

In the meantime, Meera had opened a cola bottle and poured us two glasses. I took a sip as Yamini served our meal. 'There is more on the counter if you want,' she said, slipping her jacket on. 'I'll leave you two alone, but can come back tomorrow to clean up, so you don't have to worry about it.'

With that, she left. Meera and I dove into the deliciously spiced meal, shovelling in forkfuls between going over last-minute questions and concerns about tomorrow's trip. After dinner, we abandoned our empty plates and curled up together on my sofa. Meera pulled her hair out of her ponytail, knowing how much I loved playing with her soft locks.

Running my fingers through her hair, we talked about the future, both our future and the future of Musafir. Curious as I was to know if Meera had decided to marry me, we avoided the subject. I didn't want to ruin the night by making her uncomfortable again. Life needs compromise. In goals, in love, and in your dreams. But in the end, I knew waiting for Meera to marry me would be so very worth it.

I leaned over and kissed Meera, gently at first, and then with a passion that exploded as she matched my enthusiasm. We kissed in a way that we never had before and the power of it conjured happiness I had never felt until that very moment.

My hands were tangled in her hair as our kisses deepened. I could feel her heart pounding against my chest as we pressed together, running our hands over each other, pulling even closer.

Our love was so intense, it amazed me. We journey the path to love with another, never alone, and I was certainly thriving in that love on this night.

I was awake before the sun rose the next morning, excitement and anticipation surging through my veins. In a few short hours, I would be greeting our guests for our maiden voyage for Musafir. I had checked, double checked, and triple checked all of the details, and I knew I had driven my staff half-crazy making sure they did the same.

The rational part of me knew there would be mistakes and unforeseen circumstances. Problems were sure to arise, and I wished again that Meera had been able to come with me because she was a fantastic problem solver. However, she was only a phone call away, and the effort that we all went into planning this first tour was going to keep those issues to a minimum.

And, any issues that arose? I smiled as I looked through all the appropriate documents once more, knowing that those challenges would be solved, and would be important to remember for future trips.

Yes, Musafir was ready to launch!

The sun caressed my face as I climbed out of the cab and strode to our locked office door with determined purpose. There, once more, I went through the necessary paperwork, making sure I had all the contact information for the people who would be hosting our trip.

'Vivaan!' Meera's buoyant voice broke through my thoughts and I looked up from my files, smiling broadly. 'Are you ready for your big day?'

'Aw, Meera,' I said, grateful to see her beautiful face once more before I left. 'I thought we said our goodbyes last night. You were sleeping so peacefully when I left, I didn't want to wake you. I didn't expect to see you here!'

'I couldn't let you leave without being here to wave to your bus as it leaves!' she laughed, crossing back to the window to peer out of the glass. 'When will the bus be here?'

I walked around the office and looked out the window, wrapping my arms around her and resting my chin on the top of her head. Her hair was still damp from her shower, and the flowery scent of her shampoo even stronger than usual.

'Any minute,' I responded. 'I asked him to come about an hour before we leave so I can give the driver some last-minute instructions. I figure we should have a solid half hour to go through the details yet again before the customers start to arrive. I asked them to come about thirty minutes before we leave.' I pressed my lips on the top of her head and gave her a loud, exaggerated kiss.

'I'll miss you, Vivaan.' She leaned against me even harder, squeezing my arms possessively.

'You know I'll miss you too,' I responded. 'I'll be in touch every night and I'll text you after we leave to let you know how things are going.'

'Perfect,' she murmured. 'Oh! I almost forgot!'

Meera darted out of my arms, spinning around to face me as she pulled something out of her bag.

I smiled. 'A gift?'

'It's nothing much,' she said dismissively. 'But I wanted to give you something to commemorate your first trip.'

I slid off the ribbon and tore off the wrapping paper. There, in a small box, was a beautiful, heavy, navy blue pen. I pried it out of the cushioning and examined it. 'It's beautiful,' I said, touched. On one side of the pen, my name was engraved in steel grey letters. On the other side was our company's name. Musafir.

'The perfect travelling instrument for my traveller,' she said.

'Thank you so much,' I breathed and hugged her once more. 'It is perfect,' I confirmed, leaning down to kiss her soft lips.

We were still sharing that amazing kiss when I heard the rumbling of a diesel engine driving by the office slowly. I broke the kiss and grinned down at Meera. 'I believe our chariot has arrived!' I looked up and, sure enough, the tour bus was just pulling in.

Realizing that I was still holding the pen, I rushed back to my desk, deposited the box on top of my desk and took out my soft briefcase. I took out the disposable pen that I had already put in the pen holder and slid my gift in its place. I quickly slid my paperwork back into the satchel and zipped it closed.

'It's show time,' I said, just as our driver pushed open the door.

'Dev Sarthi at your service,' the small, white-haired man said, introducing himself to Meera before giving me a mock salute. 'The bus is full of diesel and we are ready to go.' He laughed a giant, bubbly laugh.

We shared a chuckle as I reached out and shook his hand before introducing Meera. 'This is my....' I broke off. For a fleeting moment, I wished I could introduce her as my fiancée, but ... not yet. 'This is my girlfriend,' I said. Inwardly, I frowned. That title was so inadequate.

Dev's chatter broke any discomfort I felt, and we quickly transitioned into last-minute details.

We were just wrapping up when the clients arrived. First, a couple, then a single older woman, and then the rest of the group came in all at once, with a jumble of conversation and baggage.

It took a little time to sort out the suitcases. Looking at all the similar ones, I was glad one of my staff members had suggested that we purchase reusable luggage tags in bright colours and print the Musafir logo on one side. It would make it easier to identify which bag belongs to whom, and it also gave them something to use for future travels. Hopefully, the logo would catch the attention of other travellers, who would contact us and join one of our tour groups.

I took a quick roll call as we loaded up on the bus. I had placed my bag on one of the front seats, so nobody would sit there, and Karan, my trusted sidekick at Musafir, sat beside me.

Frowning, I realised one person was missing. 'Does anybody know Shridhar Laghari?' I asked the group. Our fellow travellers looked from one to the other, but everyone shook their heads slowly. I stepped on the bus to pull out my satchel once again to locate his phone number. Just then, I heard a car's engine downshifting quickly and a red sports car squealed into the parking lot.

'I'm guessing this is our elusive guest,' Dev said dryly.

A tall man jumped out of the car and waved enthusiastically. 'So sorry I'm late!' he called across the parking lot as he trotted to the back of the car and pulled out his bag. 'Thanks for waiting!'

I looked him over with a slightly annoyed eye, trying to size him up. Hopefully, he wouldn't make it a habit of being late throughout the trip. Meera caught my eye and smiled broadly; my cue to lighten my own facial expression. He is a paying customer, after all. I put on what Meera called my 'banker's smile'... perhaps not as genuine as it could have been, but it was the best I could muster at the moment.

'You just made it,' I said, trying to keep my annoyance out of my tone. A quick glance to Meera proved I wasn't quite successful. *Oh well, it was best that he is aware that we are on a schedule*, I thought.

'Perfect!' he said, ignoring the censorious timbre of my voice.

Meera had already written out his name tag and handed it me silently. I watched Shridhar sizing her up and, for one brief moment, was glad she wasn't going on the trip. I didn't care for the way he was looking at her.

'Your larger bag will have to go into the hold,' I said, handing him the tag. He looked worried for a quick second; a look that was gone as quickly as it had appeared on his face.

'This bag has my laptop though,' he said. 'I can keep that with me, right?'

I nodded. 'Absolutely.'

'Very good,' he said, climbing on to the bus.

I started to say goodbye to Meera once more when I

noticed that Shridhar had a funny look on his face. 'Is anything wrong?' I asked him.

He trotted back down the steps and whispered, 'I get motion sickness sometimes. I'm not sure the back of the bus would be a good place for me.'

I felt a wave of pity for the man; after all, he looked so vulnerable for a moment. 'Okay,' I said and climbed back on the bus. I looked at all the empty seats near the front of the bus, but the logical solution was to ask Karan to move back. Luckily, he was happy to accommodate my request, and Shridhar took the now-empty seat beside me, moving my satchel to the aisle seat.

This might be a long trip, I thought to myself.

I hugged Meera goodbye one last time and climbed the bus again. Dev closed the doors behind me and I felt the wash of air conditioning envelop me. I hadn't realised how hot I was, and I gave him a quick nod in thanks.

After a few last-minute instructions, I let them know where our first stop would be. 'There is a restaurant there,' I said. 'We can have a quick bite to eat, but it will be a few hours. You all had breakfast already, right?' I saw enough nods to satisfy my concern.

Finally, the bus pulled away from the curb and I leaned around my seat companion to wave to Meera. It might have been rude, but the man did take my seat, after all.

Fortunately, Shridhar turned out to be a decent travelling companion, chatting happily about his life and reasons for taking this trip. Despite his rocky start, I was starting to enjoy the guy.

At our first stop, he was gracious to the other passengers, and I could see them softening towards him as well. I sent a quick text to Meera, knowing she was probably concerned about the rocky departure. She responded within a minute and I knew she must have been watching her phone, waiting for me to reach out.

The rest of the day went smoothly, and I almost felt a sense of euphoria as I sat back, mulling over the amazement that my dream was coming true. My future was unfolding in front of me, spreading her arms to welcome me into this new chapter of my life.

We were at a petrol pump, fuelling up the bus near the Gujarat-Rajasthan border. It was a quick stop, so I asked people to stay on the bus, so we could push through the last few hours before we stopped for the night. We had already eaten our meal and as Dev climbed off the bus, I stood and looked over my guests. Everyone was reclining comfortably in their seats, satiated by a fantastic dinner and happy to have their hard-earned vacation in front of them.

'Boss,' Dev called through the door. 'We have company.'

I crouched and looked out the window, taking in the two police officers approaching the bus. I wasn't surprised; my contacts had told me that in this area, the authorities often checked vehicles to make sure there were no problems. I wasn't worried; guards at the Gujarat–Rajasthan border had already checked our bus. Nothing could have changed after we left the border.

I pulled my satchel from the floor, set it on the seat and opened it to take out the necessary paperwork, identifying my company and my passengers. I wasn't sure what they might ask for, but I wasn't concerned. My staff had made sure I had all the proper certification in an event such as this.

Pulling out my pen, I took that and the paperwork and climbed down the steps to greet the police officers. They were amicable enough, and I invited them on to the bus to talk to our passengers before they even asked.

Standing outside with Dev, I let the officers check everyone's identification and check bags.

My first sense that something was wrong was when one of the officers left the bus with my satchel in his hand. 'Is this yours, sir?' he asked in a serious tone.

Immediately, I began to get nervous. I knew it was foolish, because I had nothing to hide. But the look on his face told me a problem was imminent. My mind was racing. What could he have thought he found? 'Yes,' I said. 'Is there a…'

'Come with me,' he said forcibly.

We walked to the police car together, his hand firmly clutching my arm.

At first, I was completely numb when he reached into my bag with a gloved hand and pulled out a package. 'What is that?' I asked stupidly.

'I'd like you to tell me,' he said.

I shook my head slowly. 'I have no idea what this is,' I said. 'I've never seen that before.'

He barked a sharp laugh, more of a snort, and my stomach turned over as realisation came over me in waves of disbelief, terror, and helplessness.

Still, there was a feeling of disconnect as I was loaded into the police car and driven to the police station. The feeling that I was watching a bad movie continued as I was booked for drug possession. It made me sick to think of the PR this would garner in the papers. It would be bad. Very bad.

Who could have done this? I frowned, mentally going over my passenger list. Who would have wanted to hurt me like this?

I sat on the hard, concrete bench in the jail, staring at the wire-covered lightbulb until my eyes burned. Around me, I heard people yelling, but I didn't hear words. All I could hear was my own voice asking, 'Why?'

Finally, I was allowed to call Meera. Tears were streaming down my face when I told her what the police found.

Musafir wasn't even twenty-four hours old and all my dreams had come to a screeching halt.

15

FATE

I bet you didn't see that coming, did you?

Neither did Vivaan.

Did you honestly think those drugs were his? Unfortunately, for him, the police did. So did a lot of other people.

Remember Shridhar? Perhaps it would have been better for everyone if he had missed the bus. The drugs were his! When Vivaan left the bus to talk to the police, Shridhar slipped his drugs into Vivaan's bag.

You see, before you rejoin this little story, let me have the pleasure of telling you that Vivaan's company folded, and he had to lay off his employees. I loved seeing the pain in his eyes when he told his staff they lost their jobs. He had to refund the money for the failed trip and he couldn't even pay them for the time they put in.

His faithful Meera did come the next day to bail him out of jail. She didn't scold or question him, even though she had a million questions. But he had no answers for her.

How sad.

But you have to admit, it's amazing how I can turn the tables so quickly. I'm sure you think I'm done with them, and I'm going to put them back on their silly, happily-ever-after path.

You may be forced to wrestle with the truth or fight to get what you want in life, but that doesn't mean that you can be labeled a fighter.

Nothing remains the same. The person you said goodbye to in the morning will be slightly different in the evening. That is the way life moves on.

We all lose something. We lose loved ones, we lose opportunities. We can't get these things back, but that is part of life. It is difficult to lose, but there is no one in the world who can win everything, always.

No matter how contented you are in life, change is inevitable. You can't predict where or when it's going to happen and no matter how systematically careful you are in planning out your life, you can't live in a bubble without outside influences.

It's those influences that push and pull at you. Sometimes, they create possibilities; other times, they create strife.

I'm not going to lie to you. I love it when things go off track. No matter how smooth the road is, there are obstacles. There are animals that dart out in front of your car and you have to crank on the steering wheel to miss them. Sometimes it ends well for you and that animal; other times, you have a destroyed car.

It happens so fast, you can't predict the outcome. You can't predict if you're going to come out unscathed, or if you will end up with a broken car and a smashed animal. Yuck.

But that is what life is all about! It's about those split decisions! It's about reaction times and moving quickly and making decisions in a heartbeat that may impact the rest of your life.

Take it from me, though. Never, ever say, 'Life can't get any worse.' Because it can.

16

MEERA

Since the day Vivaan left for his first trip, I woke up every single morning with a burning pit in my stomach. Before my eyes even opened, I saw a vision of my dear boyfriend, staggering out from the police station after I bailed him out.

Seeing him that way nearly broke my heart, a heart that had its share of kicks lately. First Kabir's injury, and losing his beloved café. Then, Vivaan and the drug fine.

Fortunately, I was able to access the money in my bank quickly since a substantial royalty cheque had just arrived a few days ago.

If there is anything positive about the situation, it's that the drugs in his bag were less than ten grams, so he only had to pay a fine instead of serving jail time. After the stories that he told me about his night in prison, I was thankful that he wasn't found with more drugs, which would have been a non-bailable offense. But that was little consolation when I saw this ghost of a man after he was arrested.

At the police station, part of me wanted to beat his chest with clenched fists. How could he allow something like this to happen? He was so excited about starting Musafir... how could he leave any little thing to chance?

But as I drove through the night to reach Vivaan where he had been arrested, I knew that wasn't fair. His dream was shattered. As the darkness pressed on my car in the early morning hours, I gave myself permission to sort through all these feelings. I was furious with him for a while. Then I was scared.

My car was rolling into the police station parking lot when I resigned myself to whatever fate might be handing us.

I sat behind my steering wheel for a few more minutes. I was anxious to get Vivaan out of that horrible place, but I needed to make sure my own emotions were in place before I saw him. The last thing I wanted to do when I saw him was burst into tears.

Steeling myself, I pulled out my purse and systematically counted the money to make sure I had the right amount. I didn't want to stay there any longer than I had to. I was determined to go in, pay the money, and wait for Vivaan to be brought out to me.

A few tears snuck out after we finally left the police station. In the car, Vivaan leaned his tousled head against the seat and closed his eyes for a second. I could sense that he wanted to look at me, but he couldn't. Instead, he blindly reached out and took my hand.

'I'm sorry,' he said.

We drove back to Pune in silence. He was lost in his thoughts and I turned my mind to my book. I had written about half of it, when the thoughts just stopped flowing. They dried up like a stream under the hot sun.

I was trying not to panic, but between what happened with Kabir and then helping Vivaan get Musafir started, I had already lost precious time working on my book. This despite Aashi helping out the whole time, either with my work or with my friends, so I could focus on writing, which was a struggle. Now, I knew I would have to turn in a full manuscript in three months, and there was simply nothing in my mind. I just couldn't make the words come out, and when they did, they sounded empty, hollow.

All these things played out in my head every morning before I got out of bed. I wondered if these memories were just lying in wait every night, just waiting for my defences to be down. Waiting to nudge themselves past my dreams and taint every morning.

We barely talked about that horrible day. Aside from the time that we spoke with Nisha and Kabir, the only time he would mention it was when he would give me emotionless updates on closing Musafir.

The lease was broken.

The files were packed up.

The next tour was cancelled.

The deposits had been returned.

The employees were terminated.

In small sentences, he would give me these updates and I watched helplessly as his dream was systematically taken apart.

A few nights after his arrest, he completely broke down. We were watching a movie in my apartment. I was curled up on the side of the sofa and Vivaan was stretched out across the length of the furniture with his head on my lap.

Suddenly, I felt something wet on my legs. Startled, I looked down and saw tears streaming down Vivaan's cheeks. He was crying silently, and I would never have known what was going on had his tears not seeped through my clothing.

Gently, I cupped his cheek, turning him so he had to look at me. Finally, he opened his anguished eyes.

'What are you thinking?' I whispered.

'Kafe Kabir,' he whispered back. 'Why didn't I just take my savings and help Kabir and Nisha rebuild? Now, Musafir is gone and I have no money to help Kabir.' He started to sob.

I was barely aware of sliding onto the floor, then kneeling so my face was inches away from his. I wanted desperately to brush away his tears, but I was afraid to call attention to his visible misery.

'You listen to me,' I ordered firmly. 'We'll find a way to rebuild Musafir AND Kafe Kabir. This is not the end, Vivaan. My advance will come through and we'll live carefully. Maybe you and I should think about moving in together, so we only have one set of bills to think about.'

He shook his head and took a deep breath. 'You know I would love us to move in together, but not because I've failed.'

'You have not failed.'

He barked out a bitter laugh that stabbed at my heart like a pin trying to pop a balloon. 'What would you call it, Meera? This is hardly a success. My ... my company was barely born before it died.'

'But that wasn't your fault!' I cried desperately. Suddenly, I was afraid, very afraid. Vivaan was so distraught, so disappointed in himself. I needed to make him see he was not a failure ... otherwise... He wouldn't try to run away again, would he? Or worse?

Vivaan pushed himself up on the sofa angrily. 'How can you say that? This is all my fault.'

A cold wave washed over me. 'You're not saying those drugs were yours...' I couldn't even believe the words were coming out of my mouth.

'NO!' he said sharply.

'Then what are you talking about?' I asked.

'I took this risk. I wanted to start that company. I FAILED.' By then, he was breathing hard and the tears were falling, unchecked, down his face. They seemed like angry tears to me, though, and for a minute, I relaxed. Angry was better than broken.

Vivaan pushed himself off the couch. 'I think I need to go home,' he said.

In turn, I scrambled to my feet and grabbed his arm. 'Vivaan, stay. Please,' I said desperately.

He shook his head and swiped at his tears. 'I need to think, Meera. I just need to be alone for a little while.'

I sighed and nodded. 'Will you call me when you get home? Just let me know you got home okay,' I pleaded.

He nodded, but I knew he wasn't really in the room anymore. His thoughts had taken him elsewhere. I hugged him, and for the first time, I could tell he was just going through the motions as he let me hug him. When I finally let him go, his arms fell limply to his sides and he turned to leave.

I rushed to the front window after he left and watched him leave the driveway, feeling like a part of that calm I was so carefully trying to maintain had fled with him.

With a cry, I flung myself on the floor right beside my front door. Wrapping my arms around my knees, I let my own sadness overtake me, and I rocked myself back and forth until the tears subsided.

The next morning, I didn't picture Vivaan's broken spirit when he left the police station. Instead, I relived the absent hug he had given me when we said goodnight.

Resigned, I got up and brewed a cappuccino. I was on my second cup—this time without the sugar—when my phone rang. I looked at the caller ID and smiled. It was my publisher. Things were finally going to start turning around. I already imagined calling Vivaan with the news of our agreed-upon price for my new book.

'Meera,' I heard my publisher's booming voice start, but I knew there was no good news in his tone. 'Do you have a moment to speak?'

'Of course,' I responded nervously. 'Is everything okay?'

I heard him sigh heavily on the other line. 'No, I'm afraid it isn't. Meera, I just read a disturbing article in the newspaper.'

Oh no. He heard about Vivaan.

'I can assure you, Vivaan is innocent,' I said quickly. My legs started to shake, and I sat down heavily on the chair behind my desk.

'Whether he is or not is not the matter here,' he said in return.

I bit my lip. 'What do you mean?'

Another sigh. 'Meera. I like you. You're a very talented woman and your books have been a boon to our company.'

'But?' I whispered, my stomach churning.

'But you are listed in the newspaper as a co-owner of that company.'

'I don't understand. I'm not being accused of anything,' I said, confused.

'No, you're not,' he confirmed. 'However, you need to understand that your name has some negative associations right now. Your name is being connected with a drug arrest, no matter how fair or unfair that is for you.'

'What are you saying?' I was barely able to ask past the burning in my throat.

I heard him clear his throat. 'Meera, I don't know how to say this. Your competitors are taking advantage of the bad PR and are suggesting that you lack morals, and that makes them question every character in your books.

'I just don't understand,' I said weakly.

'Our company needs to distance ourselves from you. Meera, I cannot honour our agreement.'

I stood up so quickly, the backs of my knees pushed the chair into the wall. 'But we had a deal!'

'No, we didn't,' my publisher replied. 'No contract was signed. We are walking away from our agreement. I hope I'm wrong—'

'You are wrong!'

His calm tone made me even angrier when he spoke. 'I'm sure I am,' he said in a placating tone. 'But we cannot move forward with you.'

Sometime later, I realised I was still standing behind my desk with my phone still in my hand. We had long since ended the call, but I couldn't move enough to even put my phone down.

'Meera?' I heard Aashi's voice call from the front door where she let herself in. I didn't respond, and she finally poked her head into my office. 'There you are!' she said before the look on my face registered. 'What's wrong?' my faithful assistant asked.

I finally sat down, defeated. 'My contract was cancelled.'

She gasped. 'What? Why?'

'The publishers saw an article in the paper. About Vivaan. And since my name is associated with the company, suddenly I am a liability. They cut me loose.'

For the longest time, we sat in silence, both absorbing the ramifications. I remembered what I had said to Vivaan the night before. Any hope I had left was tied to that advance. Devastation washed over me and for the first time, even though I thought I understood what Vivaan had been feeling, I realised how defeating these accusations were.

'May I make a suggestion?' Aashi finally ventured tentatively.

I looked at her, forgetting she had even been in the room with me. Blinking my eyes to pull out of my stupor, I tried to collect my thoughts. Although every part of my being wanted to shriek and wail, I tried to cling to Aashi's calm demeanour.

'I hope you have a better idea than I do,' I said miserably. 'Because I don't see any way out of this.'

'Well... there are many more publishers in India,' she said. 'Let's make a list of the top ones and you can reach out to them. Let them know you're free to pursue other contracts. Before you know it, they'll be lining up outside your door, begging to sign you.'

I pursed my lips. Of course, what she said made sense. Not the part about begging to sign me, I thought dryly, but the part about there being other options for me.

Over the next week, Aashi and I made phone calls,

created pitch letters, and reached out. I begged her not to tell Vivaan what was going on—I wasn't confident that he could handle more bad news—and we charged through the top list of publishers.

Then, we started to reach out to the next tier, those that hadn't made the top of our list.

I watched Aashi's face carefully one day as she took yet another call. The hopeful look she had when the phone rang quickly dissolved into disappointment. 'Thank you for letting us know,' she said weakly and hung up the phone.

'Cross another off the list?' I guessed, and Aashi nodded.

'Cross another off what list?' I jumped, hearing Vivaan's voice. Neither of us heard him come in. 'What's going on?' he asked, looking pointedly at Aashi and me.

I ignored the question for a second. 'Aashi, would you mind warming up my cappuccino?' I asked her calmly. With a little squeak, she took my cool cup and scurried out of the room.

I walked around my desk slowly, trying to figure out how to tell Vivaan what was going on. Somehow, he seemed to know, though. He leaned against my desk, pulled me into his arms, and held me as I told him the whole story.

17

KABIR

Being a burn victim is unlike anything I would have ever imagined. When the fire stripped the flesh off my body, surviving the trauma was only the first step. It's not like a broken bone or a sprained ankle—those things can heal. Yes, I was healing, but I knew I would never be the same again.

'Kabir,' Nisha said, coming into the room, Jianna planted firmly on her hip. 'Would you like to go out for a walk today? The weather is so beautiful, and I thought it would be nice to go to the park and have a picnic lunch. It's warm, but not too hot and it's overcast so the direct sun won't hurt your scars.'

I wanted to say yes, to keep the sparkle in her eyes, but today was a bad day, pain wise. Plus, my heart was heavy for Vivaan and Meera. Hearing that Meera had lost her publishing contract was just one more weight that tugged at my heart. I could barely muster the energy to walk into the kitchen, never mind walking to the park.

I shook my head sadly. 'I don't think so, not today,' I responded.

As I anticipated, the smile left her eyes, and disappointment set in once more. It seemed like all I could do lately was disappoint the woman I loved.

Ironically, now that I was forced to lay around and heal, I realised that I had missed out on so much because I was busy either building Kafe Kabir or making it better. The woman I shared my life with, the one I pledged to take care of, had spent many lonely days and evenings here, without me. She ran the house alone when I should have been at her side more.

Now that I was here, I could barely scrape up the energy to smile around the pain. I frowned at the scar on my hand. Wounds can be covered with scars, but some open up the moment they are touched with the wrong words. I think Nisha knew that, judging by the way she spoke so carefully these days.

She now sat down beside me, repositioning our baby on her lap. 'Are you okay?' she asked, concern wrinkling her brow. 'Is the pain bad today?'

I nodded. 'Yes, and Nisha, I just feel so bad for Vivaan and Meera. They had their dreams, and those bright goals were going to bring them success, I just know they would. It's so unfair. Plus, I feel even worse because they had such hopes of helping us. I think it put even more pressure on them, so their failures must seem even greater to them.'

Nisha smiled sadly. 'I've thought of that too. I want to tell them that they haven't let us down, not at all. But how do you go about saying something like that?'

My shoulders lifted in a shrug, as much as they could with the tight scarring around that area.

Sensing our despondency, or maybe because she was a rambunctious two-year-old, Jianna began to squirm in Nisha's lap. 'I know, baby,' Nisha soothed.

'Why don't you take her to the park for a couple hours?' I suggested.

'Oh,' Nisha demurred, 'I don't know if that's a good idea. I don't want to leave you alone. We'll just stay here.' As if she understood our conversation, Jianna started to screw up her face and tears threatened.

'I'll be fine,' I insisted. 'It's only for a few hours and I think I'll just take a nap anyway. It feels like that is what my body wants right now.'

She looked hesitant, torn. I could tell she wanted to go but wanted to stay with me at the same time. I smiled encouragingly. 'Are you sure?' she said hesitantly, chewing her lip. 'Maybe just an hour.'

'Enjoy yourself,' I said. 'I'll see you after my nap.' To emphasise my decision, I shifted positions and laid my head on the arm of the couch. She stood up quickly and I pulled my legs up and stretched out where she had been sitting.

I heard her humming quietly as she gathered the diaper bag and the stroller. It was nice to hear that happy sound from her. 'Call me if you need me,' she insisted, closing the door behind her quietly.

After she left, I got up and shuffled over to the window, standing far enough from the window so she couldn't see me if she looked over, but close enough so I could watch my small family walking down the street. Her step seemed lighter, and I knew she was probably relieved to be out of the house for a little while.

She turned around a corner and I returned to the couch, sitting down heavily. The burns on my arms hurt, but seeing her happily walking down the street made my heart ache even more.

Sweet Nisha. She had always been there for me, waiting patiently for each next phase of our life. When we met, her spirit had been shattered and I had tried to coax a smile out of her with a cold coffee and ice cream. I was only working at a café at the time, but even with only a handful of words between us, I started to dream about this beautiful woman in the coral dress.

But, I mused on the couch, Nisha was still waiting. I was busy with the café and my long hours were driven by my desperate need to ensure my family's comfort. I didn't want Nisha and our baby wanting for anything. And, until Kafe Kabir went up in flames, they didn't want for anything.

Except for my time and attention.

I was crushed as I came to the realisation that they had been hungry for me. Husband. Father.

I was standing by the door as it clicked open and Nisha tiptoed in with a sleeping, sweaty baby on her shoulder.

'What are you doing?' she whispered.

'Why don't you put her down?' I suggested, also in a low tone. 'I want to talk to you.'

She nodded, her eyes darting around the apartment like she was looking for something out of place. I trailed behind her, tiptoeing into our room where the cot was waiting. Gently, Nisha sat on the edge of the small bed and carefully settled the baby on to the cool sheets, her eyes searching Jianna's face to make sure she wasn't waking up.

I stood beside Nisha, my arm draped over her shoulders. She sat up and leaned into me for a moment. We held hands and watched the calm breaths of our sleeping child for several long moments. Then, I stepped away from Nisha and tried to tug her to her feet. My strength was still not there, but I didn't have to try too hard because the next thing I knew, she was pushing herself into my arms. By now, she knew where it hurt when she touched me, and her arms went confidentially around my undamaged skin.

Silently, we broke our embrace and left the slumbering Jianna.

I tugged Nisha out of the bedroom and closed the door behind us. 'Can you come into the living room?' I whispered.

'Kabir?' my wife said, looking at me with intense curiosity.

I didn't really know where to start; my throat was a logjam of emotions. But I needed to start somewhere. We sat on the edge of the sofa, so our knees were touching. I sighed and took a breath to speak. But the words still didn't come out.

Finally, I managed two words. 'Forgive me.' And I crumpled into her arms, the tears flowing freely. Bless Nisha, she said nothing, but she let me cry, rocking me gently in her loving, warm embrace. Our Jianna was the luckiest little girl to have such a nurturing mother. I could feel the love radiating from her as she held me.

When my tears were finally spent, I pulled away, but I couldn't look her in the eye. Instead, I stared at the floor miserably.

'Forgive you for what?' she finally asked.

Finally, I dragged my eyes up to hers, locked in her intense stare.

'For what?' she repeated. 'I don't understand.'

I took a deep, shuddering breath. 'You have been by my side for a very long time now,' I began, reaching out and lacing my fingers with hers. 'From the time you and I were engaged, you loved me and supported me, even though all my conditions.'

Nisha frowned. 'Conditions?'

'Unspoken ones,' I said sadly. 'I didn't even realise it until now. The condition that I couldn't marry you until I could support you. Then the condition that I had to work hard to make Kafe Kabir a success. I put in long hours, and never once did you complain.

'Nisha, I have neglected you,' I said bluntly. 'I've been so busy, too busy to give you what you deserved: me.'

She laughed a little nervously. 'You've had so much on your mind.'

'Forgive me?' I said again.

Tenderly, Nisha reached out and brushed an errant tear from my cheek. 'There is nothing to forgive. I love you,' she said simply.

Those simple words were a balm to my aching spirit. There was still a heaviness in my heart though, and I knew Nisha could sense it.

'Something else is worrying you,' she guessed.

I shook my head angrily. 'I've been so stupid,' I said.

'All these years, I've put the café first. I worked so hard, ignoring you... and what do I have to show for it?'

'I don't understand.'

'The café is gone, destroyed. We don't have the money to rebuild and my hospital bills have taken everything else. My biggest fear when we were engaged has come true. After everything, I'm right back where I started,' I said, starting to cry again. 'I can't support you and Jianna. I am nothing, yet again.'

If I thought she was going to take me in her arms and soothe me again, I was very wrong. 'No!' she said sharply, her eyes flashing with anger. 'You are not nothing, Kabir! You are a loving husband and father.'

'Who hasn't been there.'

'Who is here now.'

I heaved a sigh. 'And I promise you that I will never put work before my family again. Ironic now that I have no way of making a living,' I said bitterly.

Once again, her face creased into a smile. 'I haven't been sure how to mention this,' she started. 'But I've been putting away a little money.'

'From where?'

'Oh, just from the household expenses, a little bit here and there,' she said dismissively. 'It wasn't that hard.'

I grinned. 'You are an amazing woman.'

'It's not a lot,' Nisha clarified. 'But it will take care of things for the next few months, while you continue to heal, and we figure out how to rebuild.'

Relief flooded me. In one conversation, she had calmed my fears in so many ways. She was truly the most amazing woman, and she was my wife. With her by my side, we would be okay.

18

MEERA

'Vivaan,' I said, hating my voice. It sounded weak. 'Please, don't push me away.'

I heard a short laugh on the other end of the phone. 'Meera, you're overreacting. I'm not pushing you away. I just need to do some things tonight, so I can't come over.'

What do you have to do? Sit there in your dark apartment and feel sorry for yourself? Because that seems like it's all that you do! I screamed the words in my head, but I managed to keep them in. I knew they would only hurt him.

'I am not overreacting,' I insisted. 'You've grown more and more distant. I barely see you anymore.'

He heaved a sigh and I could hear a lot of background noise on the phone like he was tapping something against the counter.

'I'll see you tomorrow.'

'You said that yesterday.'

'Meera, I mean it. I'll see you tomorrow. Please don't give me a hard time,' he said, weariness in his voice.

'I love you,' I said, but I knew the words were just that: words. What good was love when it ripped through you and poured tears into your heart?

'Love you,' he said absently and hung up.

I looked at my phone for a long time before I placed it on the desk beside my manuscript.

I scowled at the page, which was mostly empty. There were exactly two full paragraphs. The third one was half empty. The final sentence wasn't even completed. I dropped my head in defeat. It wasn't even that I was interrupted by Vivaan's phone call mid-sentence. I stopped writing twenty minutes before he even called. The sentence was incomplete because the words were just gone.

Can I even call myself a writer anymore? I thought desperately. *Why am I even torturing myself with a book that won't sell?*

It was just one more thing on my mind. Two days ago, I had to release Aashi from her duties. After pouring so much money into Musafir, I had to cut back on my own expenses just to keep moving forward.

I adored Aashi and she had always been there for me, but I couldn't ask her to work for me without paying her. She had her own expenses too, and I needed to release her, so she could find another job.

I wept as I hugged her that day. 'I will always be here for you, Meera,' she said, tears in her eyes too. 'I know this is only temporary. You'll start writing again, I know. It is in your blood. Just remember I'm only a phone call away if you need me.'

Even now, I doubted the wisdom of letting Aashi go. Maybe tomorrow things would change, and I would start writing again.

But you can't buy food on maybes.

Besides, even if I did start writing again, even if the words started tumbling out even faster than I could write them, who would want to buy my book? I had plunged from the top-selling female writer to nothing. I couldn't believe how cruel people could be. Authors that I met at the lit fest, people whose hands I shook, were flinging venom at my name just to promote their own work.

They had morals, they said, suggesting that I didn't.

Morals? Ha! They lied just to push their name out there. They couldn't do it on their talent, could they?

'That's just mean, Meera,' I scolded myself. 'You are not that person.'

I picked up my phone again, needing to get out of the house and away from these destructive, negative thoughts. I needed people around me. I climbed into my car and started towards Nisha and Kabir's place.

19

VIVAAN

I couldn't stand to be in the city anymore. Everywhere I turned, I felt there were signs of my failure. I couldn't go near the neighbourhood where my office was located. The area, the restaurants, everything reminded me of those hopeful days when things seemed so promising.

I avoided Meera, barely able to take in that brave smile masking the devastation she must have felt.

Honestly, if I could have, I probably would have run halfway around the world again. But I couldn't afford a plane ticket to the next state, never mind travelling abroad.

But I still had my car, and I could still buy petrol, for a little while longer, anyway. I slid into my faithful vehicle and started to drive.

As the tall buildings of Pune shrunk in my rear-view mirror, I began to breathe a little easier. I didn't know where I was going, but I did know I couldn't turn around and go back any time soon.

It wasn't until I was passing by buildings on either side of NH48 that I was starting to get a sense of where I might be going. It wasn't a deliberate trek, but more of a pull like I was being drawn to a certain region.

The pull started to get stronger as I turned onto SH65 and saw the Siddhi Vinayak Hospital. Memories rushed at me—this wasn't the hospital that Meera was taken to when she had her accident, but the building reminded me of those horrible, terrifying days.

I kept driving, pushing my car, seeking open spaces. The road started to wind, and I had to put both hands on my steering wheel, turning my attention to my driving. For a few minutes, I felt a relief from my own torment as my focus was on the twisting, turning road ahead of me.

Then, my car took a hard left turn. Sure enough, I was on the Rajgad Fort Road, just as I suspected. I knew what was up ahead and I looked forward to the challenge.

Yes, there it was. The Balekilla Road. It ushered in the entrance to Rajgad Fort, where Meera had fled the day I told her about my past; the news that my bride was killed on our wedding day nearly tore Meera apart. Knowing that she came here to escape her misery, it followed that I would trail her years later to escape my own misery.

Life was so unfair, and I hurled this phrase at the heavens as I started the trek to the summit. Those drugs weren't mine! I didn't deserve the speculation and the negativity. All I wanted to do was turn my own wonderment with our country into a way to support myself and Meera, if she ever chose to marry me. If that was even an option anymore, I thought bitterly as my feet pounded determinedly on the earth.

The open, green fields soon dissolved into a considerable hike and at the pace I had set my lungs started to burn with the effort it took to ascend the Murumbadevi Dongar Hills. Looking up at the steep incline ahead of me, it wasn't hard to see why this fort was difficult for enemies to attack. Captured? Yes, it fell, but not without a struggle.

I wished I had the fortitude to fight the injustices against me, but I toppled with very little effort. Perhaps I wasn't strong enough. Maybe I didn't really want to succeed.

These thoughts taunted me as I rushed up the path. At times, I felt like I was fleeing my very failure, running away from my shame. And, for a few footsteps at a time, I could escape. My mind refocused on other things… Meera's beautiful face… Kabir's smile the day he opened his own café… My thoughts would settle on happy thoughts and I could feel a few heartbeats of relief.

But then the burning in my lungs would be too much and I'd have to stop to catch my breath. And, like an enemy catching up with me, my disgrace, dogging me this whole time, would catch up and nearly overwhelm me.

My mind would taunt me with other images. As I sat there, gasping for breath, the white, carefully constructed walls of the jail cell I was unceremoniously thrown into on the first day of Musafir's premier tour especially taunted me. I heard the metal door shut firmly, determined to barricade me from the dream I was living only a few hours before.

That long, horrible night, I lay on a thin mattress on a concrete bed in the jail, miserably curled into myself. I was so distressed after being caught with drugs that weren't mine. How did that happen? I asked myself again for the hundredth time. I hated feeling helpless, but that was how I felt that night. I was stripped of everything, from my own clothes to my dignity.

As the weeks went by, the only plausible explanation was that Shridhar must have slipped the drugs into my bag. At first, I dismissed the thought because it was so unfair to accuse another person of something they didn't do ... even if the accusation was only in my mind.

But his name continued to persist in my heart, and the more I thought of it, the more I was convinced that it must have been Shridhar. He watched me being accused of something I didn't do and left me to pay for his crime. What was my crime? Not taking my satchel with me when I left the bus. Stupidity, nothing more!

Part of me wanted to verbalise the accusation and call the police, but what purpose would it serve, really? It would only keep my name in the newspapers. Even if I was right and even if Shridhar admitted to the crime, the PR would still bring up that horrible night, and the details of my fall from grace.

I thought I was defeated that night; I didn't realise I could fall further from grace, but I could, and I took my beloved Meera with me as I tumbled downwards. Misery pressed against me, heavy hands pushing and pulling as I struggled for every breath on the path to Rajgad Fort.

Finally, I crested the summit, my thighs burning with the effort of my half spring up the steep slopes. Maybe at the top, I thought, I would see clarity in the thin air. I would be handed the wisdom of why I was being tested, why the help I promised to Kabir was torn away from me. Why Meera's own living was suddenly undermined by that horrible day.

If I thought it was going to come as I stood, vulnerable in front of the fort gates, I was wrong. No consoling ideas came to me, no out-of-the-box thinking to dig myself out of this horrible mess.

The winds pressed against me from all four directions, wiping the sweat from my body for a few minutes before quickly instilling a numbing chill on my limbs. I didn't realise it was going to be this cold that day.

My head felt as numb, as disjointed as I felt my extremities becoming. If my arms and legs were defeated by the cold, and my mind was going too, what was next? My heart? My soul? I looked around, panicked, expecting to see some crazed enemy from centuries ago readying to take his death blow. I was sure I was dying.

But it never happened. My heart kept beating and my arms, quivering with cold and exhaustion, kept moving, rubbing the other to provide some comforting warmth. And my head kept racing with memories of caustic, defeated dreams, once so happy, but now turning against me like a family pet that unknowingly developed rabies. I was contented once, but those feelings were made even more despondent with the misery I was handed.

Slowly, I made my way to Chor Darwaja, the very same

path that I knew Meera attempted that day ... and she failed, falling down the steep stairs, almost losing her life.

Was I tempting destiny? Was I challenging it to bring its worst to me? Or was I on that very same path ... expecting it to best me?

I didn't know.

My legs were shaking with fatigue as I pictured Meera's tiny feet climbing the same steps. She told me later she climbed quite a way before she realised she was wrong to run away and she turned away to come back to me.

'I felt like I could touch heaven from there,' she told me in the hospital, several weeks into her recovery. Could I do the same? Could I touch heaven?

I turned around, taking in the amazing vista below me. It truly was awe-inspiring, as dangerous as the path may have been. I might not have been able to reach to heaven from here, but I definitely could sense its presence all around me.

I sat down on the cold, damp, grey step in front of me. And waited for absolution.

I should have felt peace like Meera did. But I still felt the weight of losing my dreams.

A small group approached me, slowly ascending to find the 'hidden door'. Scooting over on the cold step, I let them pass, determined to make eye contact with each one as they approached.

'Almost there?' one man gasped as he entered my view.

I nodded. 'Taking a break myself,' I said. 'But you're almost there.'

They passed, and I waited until the gentle, breathless murmurs of the climbing party disappeared behind a small bend.

Slowly, I stood, the weight of my failure making me feel a gazillion times heavier. I could have been on the summit of Everest, hemmed in by my own misery, my oxygen tanks depleted, and a snowstorm rushing towards me to force me off the path.

I fought the feeling and stood straight on the step where I had sat.

I took a breath. And then another one.

I looked at the steep steps below me, the ones Meera had fallen down. But I was sure she had tried to protect her body as she plummeted down, and that was why she lived.

What if I didn't fight it? What if I opened my arms and welcomed gravity while I stopped trying to fight fate?

My left foot tentatively rubbed against the edge of the step and I heard small pellets of earth dislodge as I tested its security.

Although the path down looked straight and sure, I knew my own path was forking. Nobody would think it odd if I fell, tumbling down from the heavens I nearly touched. I could follow that route. Or I could cling to the rail and inch my way down the slope again. But where would that path lead me? Would destiny turn once again and allow me a happy ending? Or was that safer path down the hill going to end in even more misery?

My cheeks were stinging with the tears streaming down my face as I made my decision.

20
FATE

This is deliciously wonderful! I have taken away everything that they have... their financial security, their means of living... poof! Gone! Isn't it amazing how quickly I can turn a charmed life and push it into utter misery?

But wait.

These fools still have... love? And... hope? How did that happen?

Huh. Well, they think they can escape me. But what good will these things do if they don't even have a way to support themselves.

Without financial comfort, they have nothing.

They may be fighting me right now. Me. Fate! The fools have no idea how strong I am. Even though I turned their lives into utter chaos, they still resist the path I have laid out for them.

Ah, but one can only fight for so long. Nobody can fight me for too long. I'm too powerful, and I don't need to play fair.

I wonder if they look back and think about the times when life went so smoothly for them. When things were just lined up in a straight line, ordered, happy, and predictable. Did they think then how quickly I would be able to kick at their neat, tidy lives?

It's just a scuff on my feet, really, but how quickly I can knock things down, tear apart their well-ordered lives.

Just like a child, when I start playing, I have a hard time stopping. It's so delightful to see the disarray that I can create. My own personal mud pie.

21

NISHA

'Ma!' Jianna shouted as she toddled toward her favourite red ball. I watched my little girl with amusement, seeing the wonders of her world through a set of two-year-old eyes.

Despite stress of the last few months, our little girl remained unaffected, and it was soothing to watch her antics as she mastered her running abilities.

We were at the Kamala Nehru Park once more. Although it was a little further from our apartment than some of the other parks, this was one of our favourites. Jianna loved the green animals carved from lush bushes and would crane her neck to look up at the giraffe every time we saw it.

But she particularly loved the open spaces. Just to move at full toddler speed delighted her and today she was trying to kick her ball at the same time, shrieking with delight every time she moved it a few inches.

Kabir was with me on this day, although he had opted to sit in the shade while I chased the baby around. I knew he was still uncomfortable, but he was laughing at Jianna's antics as she would wind up the ball and promptly throw it on the ground right in front of her. I was so happy to see him outside for the first time in a long while. Perhaps the fresh air would help him heal even more.

Jianna darted off the grass onto one of the stone walkways and went to kick her ball again. This time, though, she missed the red orb and her tiny foot landed the top of it, knocking her over.

The poor sweetheart let out an angry wail and I rushed over to pick her up, snuggling her close. With the other arm, I grabbed the ball and we returned to where Kabir was sitting, Jianna crying uncontrollably.

'Is she okay?' Kabir was sitting straight like he was about to launch himself off the bench to join us as I was heading back to him. By this time, Jianna was thrashing in my arms and I had to struggle to hold on to her as I joined Kabir on the freshly painted green bench.

'I'm sure she's fine,' I said soothingly. I swung Jianna's legs over mine and started to inspect for cuts and bruises. Sure enough, there was an angry scrape on her left knee. She must have landed on that knee when she lost her balance, my poor sweetheart. There wasn't much blood, but the skin was torn, and I could only imagine how much that stung.

I dug a cloth out of her bag and poured a little water on it, putting it on her knee to soothe the pain.

Soon, the crying turned to teary sniffles and finally stopped altogether.

I lifted the cloth and inspected the boo-boo. It was going to be sore, but it could have been much worse. Interested in the condition of her knee, Jianna looked down with wide eyes. 'Ow?' she said, and the understatement made both of us laugh. Then, she scooted off my knee, held her hands out for the ball, and took off. Curious, we watched her deliberately place the ball on the ground and reel back to kick it again.

'You clever, determined girl,' Kabir chuckled and I looked over at him. Just as I was going to respond, an idea started to blossom in my mind.

Never far from my mind, my thoughts turned back to Vivaan and Meera. Just like Jianna, they lost their balance in a way. So did Kabir, I mused. Everybody had their own dreams and each dream was interrupted, just like the baby's play when she tripped over her ball.

Jianna didn't give the pain of her scraped knee power

over her. She didn't let it get the best of her. Instead, he allowed some tears, but then she moved past the pain. She gained control of it, instead of letting it gain control of her.

'She's a tough one,' Kabir noted.

'Just like her daddy,' I responded and he shook his head.

'She's strong like her mommy,' he responded. 'You are my rock, Nisha.'

I wanted to comment but my mind was diverted towards Jianna when she took off running once more. What a determined little girl she was.

A small snowball of an idea started to form in my head. I started to take a breath to talk it over with Kabir, but as the sketch of this idea started to grow and take shape in my mind, I decided to keep it to myself for a while longer. The sun's rays were waning a little and Kabir joined me after I settled Jianna on a swing and started pushing her, her screams of delight drawing grins from adults around us.

By the time we packed up and headed home, Jianna's eyes were starting to droop. It was nap time. I could also tell Kabir was fighting the fatigue he so often felt in the evenings. I was sure he would be exhausted by the time we returned to our apartment on this day, one of the first times he had ventured outside.

It was hard to keep my enthusiasm down while my idea kept expanding to different possibilities, but I tempered my energy to match Kabir and Jianna's.

Kabir's sense of relief was palpable when we entered our cosy little apartment once more. I started to fuss with getting the baby ready for her nap and said nonchalantly over my shoulder, 'You look tired too, Kabir. Why don't you go and rest for some time? I have a couple of things I want to do to tidy up the living room and I don't want to keep you up.'

He groaned appreciatively and trudged into our airy

bedroom. Five minutes later, I crept in with a dozing Jianna resting on my shoulder. He, too, was out, sleeping the peaceful slumber of a man who had been out in the fresh air for the better part of a day. I settled Jianna in her cot and left the two to their naps.

I closed the bedroom door quietly, pushing the door gently so the latch would catch without a sound. Tiptoeing into the living room, I logged on to our laptop, my path clearly laid out by now.

First, I double-checked my savings account to make sure I had enough to plan my surprise. Then, I looked up a phone number and picked up my phone.

'Pari?' I confirmed when the phone connected. 'It's Nisha!'

'Nisha?' I heard in response, surprise colouring her happy voice. 'It's been too long! How are you, my friend?

I settled back and filled my childhood friend in over the last few months, patiently answering her questions as they were posted.

'And how is the little one?'

'Jianna is wonderful. I honestly can't imagine life without her. What a gift she is.'

'She sounds terrific—and growing well?'

'Very much so. She's very healthy and such a happy little girl. At first, when Kabir came home from the hospital, she seemed a little scared of all the bandages. But she soon got used to them. You know how quickly kids bounce back.'

'If only we could all bounce back that quickly.'

'I know,' I mused. And with that, it was time to tell her about my idea; a plan that hinged on what I knew to be her unerring sense of hospitality.

'I love the idea,' she purred. 'Of course, you are all welcome here! You didn't even need to ask, silly.'

I grinned. 'I know I didn't,' I said. 'You have always been a great friend. I look forward to seeing you!'

'Let me know when the plans are confirmed, and I'll see you soon.'

We hung up and for the first time in too long, I felt the warm taste of hope on my tongue once more.

Hearing Jianna on the baby monitor—she was rolling over—I glanced at the time quickly. Oh dear, I had been talking to Pari a lot longer than I expected. Hopefully, Kabir would sleep just a little longer too…

A half-hour later, I printed the tickets I had purchased and tucked them under the laptop for now.

I sent separate texts to Meera and Vivaan, asking them to come over for dinner. 'I have something important to talk to you about,' I explained in each message.

'Who are you texting?' Kabir said behind me, startling me so badly, I nearly dropped my phone. Face flushing wildly, I managed to stammer, 'I-I thought I'd… invite… Meera and Vivaan over for dinner.' I was awful at hiding surprises, and the half-truth of the invitation made me feel desperately guilty. 'Is Jianna still sleeping?' I asked. Of course, she was—she was exhausted—but I wanted to distract him while I gathered my thoughts.

'She rolled over once but she's still out,' he said absently, more curious about my reaction. He cocked an eyebrow at me but didn't comment on my obvious discomfort. 'What are we having?'

My mind went blank and then launched into a frenzied inventory of supplies in my kitchen. 'Um… I know it's kind of last minute, so something pretty quick, I'm thinking.'

Kabir grinned, settling a hip against the counter in the kitchen. 'Hm. You invite them over for dinner, but don't have dinner planned. You're stammering like a five-year-old getting caught stealing an extra biscuit… and… Nisha? You're blushing. What are you up to?'

I took a deep breath, and then let it out, weighing

the prickly discomfort of further denial, or launching the plan prematurely. Then, I squared my shoulders proudly. 'Maybe I have a surprise,' I said. 'I'll tell you when we're all together, okay?'

His chocolate brown eyes searched mine, but I could tell he was also weighing teasing me further or letting me off the hook. He smiled again, and I knew he was letting me escape ... for now.

'Do you want me to order something?' he suggested, glancing at the clock.

'No,' I decided. 'I can pull something together. We've had so many restaurant meals; I'm missing my kitchen. Why don't you go sit down?'

He nodded and turned to leave. 'Okay. Maybe I'll just go online and check—'

'No!' I said quickly, thinking of the tickets stashed under the laptop. Startled, he turned around again. I cleared my throat and held up a hand to ward off any more questions. 'It's part of the surprise. I just need you not to be on the computer right now.'

'You certainly are being mysterious today,' he said. 'May I go read a book, or is that off limits too?'

I giggled a little. 'No, that's okay,' I said, ushering him out of the kitchen.

When he was gone, I threw myself into making a nice dinner to complement the surprise I was planning to unveil to my friends. And when they came, it was indeed a nice, almost celebratory meal. We enjoyed each other's company immensely and, for a few wonderful minutes, it was like we had all been relieved of the collective burdens we all felt. The air felt lighter, positively charged.

Jianna, well rested, was playing happily after the meal. The atmosphere was perfect. No stress, nothing negative to weigh us down.

It was during those peaceful, stress-free moments at the dinner table, that I knew for sure that my plans were inspired.

As if he was reading my mind, Kabir spoke up. 'So, Nisha, what is this big secret you've been keeping all day?'

All eyes turned to me and I knew it was time for the big announcement. 'This evening, we were at the park,' I began. 'Jianna hurt her knee, but after a few tears, she got up again. After that little break, she was fine again.'

This was where things could fall apart, so I was hoping that I explained myself carefully. 'I think,' I said, taking a breath. 'No. I *know* that we all need a similar respite. Every one of us has been treaded on by fate lately. And it's been getting us down, weighing on our souls, and stealing our sleep at night.'

I looked at the other adults at the table. 'I agree,' Meera said. 'But what are you suggesting? You do seem like you have a plan.'

I laughed. 'You've always had the gift of insight,' I said teasingly. I stood up and hurried into the living room, where I had the tickets hidden. Coming in, I held them up proudly. 'We're going to take a small vacation, just for a few days.'

Vivaan pursed his lips, considering. 'I don't know, Nisha. I don't see how we can—'

Excited, I interrupted him. 'We can, and we will. I've already bought the airline tickets for all of us!'

'What?!' Meera cried, her eyes round with shock. 'Nisha! It's a nice idea… but it's too much. We… Vivaan and I… we can't accept something like this. Kabir, did you know about this?'

I wasn't sure how Kabir was reacting to the idea; his face was unreadable. Was he angry at my impulsive nature? But then he spoke, slowly, as if he were digesting the words to make sure they were appropriate before they left his mouth.

'Meera,' he said. 'I'm not going to pretend I'm not as

surprised as both of you. This is all Nisha's doing. But it's not too much, my friends. Was it too much that you both helped Nisha all those weeks since my accident? Nisha wants to return the favour, and I think it's a fantastic, inspired idea.'

'I wish I could agree,' Meera said. 'It's just bad timing. I need to focus on working.'

Just then, Jianna brought Vivaan a toy and he scooped her up in his lap.

'You're doing too much,' Kabir said. 'Every single one of us would benefit from a change of scenery.'

'I'm just not sure,' she said. 'It feels like I'm running away. It's easy to run away sometimes, but that makes it so much more difficult to return to what you fled.'

'No,' I said firmly, 'it might lend a fresh perspective for you. I think it will help your writing.'

'What if this is a mistake?'

'You can make mistakes, but you must take ownership of them,' I said, meaning a lot more than just a trip. But the words needed to be said. 'Don't blame them on destiny, or the past. Mistakes are yours, but none of us is immune to them. Take the power from them and make it your own.'

She pursed lips and nodded slowly. 'This might work.' Then she nodded more enthusiastically. 'I think you're right.'

Vivaan shook his head. 'It's just not the best time for me to leave.'

'Vivaan,' Meera said, reaching out for his hand. 'Please. I think this could be very good for all of us, but especially for you and me. It would be so good for us to step away from the things getting us down here. We need to go somewhere and start to laugh again. Please.'

He kept shaking his head and I could see the depression weighing him down. Sensing his anxiety, Jianna slid off his lap and came over to me, holding up her arms to be picked up. I picked her up and hugged her, watching Vivaan carefully. I knew his feelings well, back before I met Kabir. They were dark and tormented, every breath burning with a sense of hopelessness.

'Vivaan,' I said, using my firmest mother tone. 'You need this.'

He turned his eyes to me, surprised.

'And,' Meera continued, 'maybe it will help my writing.'

He heaved a sigh. 'I guess you're right,' Vivaan said and looked at Meera. 'I know you know I've been very depressed. And I almost let it get the best of me, just the other day.'

'What?' Meera whispered. Kabir and I exchanged a glance as Vivaan pulled together his own thoughts.

'I ended up at Rajgad Fort,' he said. 'On the path to Chor Darwaja.'

'Oh no,' his girlfriend gasped, and my heart ached to watch her fear in knowing that he deliberately chose the same path that nearly destroyed her life. 'You weren't... going to...'

Vivaan shook his head. 'I was in a bad place, emotionally,' he admitted. 'But then, standing on those steps, so close to the clouds, I knew I needed to fight the course fate had decided to set me on. However, I had no idea where to go from there.

'We don't determine how we die,' he said, 'but we can dictate how we live. So,' he said, turning his beaming grin on me, 'where is this vacation?'

The tension that unexpectedly flooded the room suddenly pulled back, like a retreating ocean wave. I grinned back, excited again. 'Goa!' I said happily.

'Oh wow,' Meera said, her face flushing with eagerness. 'I haven't been to Goa in years!' She looked over at Vivaan. 'I'm sure we can splurge for a couple days in a hotel?'

'Oh no,' I broke in. 'It won't be necessary. I took Musafir's concept and went with it.'

'Meaning what?' Vivaan asked, eyebrows lifted.

'Why stay in a hotel when we could go local? I reached out to a friend of mine who has a villa in Goa, only a few blocks from the beach. She said she has plenty of room for us to stay.'

'Everybody?' Meera gasped.

I nodded happily. 'Everybody. And she is thrilled at the idea of hosting us.'

'Nisha,' Vivaan said, 'you are an amazing friend. And friends push you to be truer to yourself than you ever could imagine without them.'

'Some things you have to accomplish by yourself; others you can't do without help,' I responded. 'You have to balance the two.'

Kabir reached over and hugged me, wincing only a little as his skin pulled tight in the sudden movement. 'I think it's the perfect idea,' he said enthusiastically. 'We can use this time to draw a line in the sand, so to speak. We will leave the past behind us, but take the time while we are there to plan for the future.'

I nodded, thrilled that everyone was so supportive of my plan. How amazing that just this morning, we were all struggling to put one foot in front of the other, plodding through our concerns, both for ourselves and each other. Now, there was a sense of anticipation flavouring our lives once again. We would take up arms against fate; we would fight it with everything we had. And when the battle was over, we would be stronger.

22

MEERA

Pari was a delightful host, welcoming us to her multi-level villa, with its smart lines and sharp angles. Kabir and Nisha took the smallest bedroom on the second floor since it was the only one without balcony, and the young parents were concerned about Jianna's curious nature.

Vivaan and I were settled on the third floor, with access to a beautiful open terrace as large as the bedrooms at one end and a smaller terrace at the back of the villa.

The moment we settled in, I could see the peace enveloping my travelling companions. I could see Vivaan looking at the surrounding area through a tour director's eyes, sizing up the possibilities in bringing guests to this region, and felt a surge of relief. Even though we had no idea how to regenerate Musafir after such a blow, I could see the pain abating.

I only hoped that it would help me with my writing. The torment of not writing was growing into this horrible monster. It followed me around wherever I went, whispering, 'Failure.' Before I left, I wrote all day and managed to produce three hundred words. Less than an article in a newspaper and that took ten hours.

And I still had no idea how it was going to impact things, even when I did finish the book. Looking at the way that publishers continued to shy away from me, I might as well set things on fire.

No, I told myself firmly, you *don't mean that. You love writing. It will love you again.*

Kabir seemed to be moving with even less pain than I observed back in Pune. The salty, moist air must have been agreeing with his scars and new skin, settling a concern that Nisha had voiced to me as we were travelling to the airport that morning.

'What if this is a mistake?' she whispered under her breath as the two men heaved the luggage out of the cab. 'I know the sun can be hard on his burns ... maybe we should have gone to the mountains instead?'

'Nisha,' I whispered back. 'Don't question yourself now. Your idea is magnificent. Look at them,' I said, nodding at the two men who were chatting happily. 'They both look like they are breathing without their burdens for the first time in too long.'

And indeed they were. The energy bounced between Kabir and Vivaan as they teased each other lightly, their eyes sparkling under the bright sun.

That relaxed nature stayed with us throughout our arrival and the first day in Goa. 'Go, write,' Vivaan said, waving me back towards my journal. 'I know you want to!'

And I did. My heart yearned for the familiar sweeping of my hand across the paper, creating images and bringing emotions to life; it was an extraordinary feeling to develop these dimensions on a flat piece of paper. I nodded to Vivaan in agreement. I pictured myself curling up comfortably on one of the chairs on the large terrace.

I chewed my lip in frustration after the others left for a trek to the beach. I wanted to write, I knew the storyline that I had carefully plotted. But like a framed house with no material to finish it, my ideas were empty, echoing in my mind.

No, I told myself. *I'm going to get some good writing done today. The fresh sea breeze will help.* Determined, I jogged up to the third floor and retrieved my journal, striding out to the terrace, challenging everything that was stopping my inspiration to defy me. Plopping myself into a chair, I turned my face to the sun, breathing in the warm, salty wind coming off the sea.

And stared at the blank page.

I got up, wandering to the edge of the terrace and leaned my hips against the strong concrete wall, looking at the street below. Maybe something down there would tease an idea out of my mind. But not now. Sometimes, words play games with you, revealing lies instead of the truth.

Frustrated, I went to my chair and threw myself down.

Knees up with my journal propped against them, I tried again. All attempts to write just felt flat, unnatural. What was happening to me? I had never felt writer's block before—I thought I was one of those people who could just wade through dry, uninspired times—but hours passed and the pages in front of me remained flat, unfeeling. The words were foreign, strangers to me ... how did they even come through my pen?

'Ugh,' I growled in frustration and decided to pad downstairs to pour a cool drink. Bless Pari, she had the kitchen well stocked and insisted that we make ourselves comfortable. 'I'll show you where everything is once,' she said. 'After that, if you remain hungry or thirsty, that is your responsibility. I'm actually a horrible hostess. I am not going to scurry after you to offer a cappuccino or freshly-baked scones. No, if you want something, I require you to help yourself!'

I loved her laid-back attitude; it made her the ideal hostess for our needs.

I was sitting at the sofa, frowning at the disjointed thoughts on the journal in front of me, when Kabir and Nisha came back with the baby asleep on Nisha's shoulder. They nodded to each other meaningfully and shared a quick kiss before Nisha tiptoed up to the second level to lay Jianna down.

'How was the beach?' I asked Kabir quietly after Nisha disappeared, her coral dress swirling around her legs.

'Hmmm?' Kabir asked and I realised that in his mind, he had followed the two up the cool steps. Perhaps it was the dress... he told me all the time it was his favourite colour on his wife.

I grinned. 'I asked how the beach was,' I repeated.

'Oh, very beautiful,' he said, his eyes still on the stairs.

'Was the sun too much?'

He shook his head. 'No, Nisha brought a huge umbrella with us, so I was able to sit in the shade. Oh, how she fussed over me. But, I'll admit, I loved every minute of it. You'd think I'd be sick of being babied by now!'

I grinned. 'I think it's called taking care of you,' I clarified. 'It's not babying.'

With a light step, Nisha descended from the second floor. Despite the heat outside, she looked fresh and content. Without even asking, Kabir handed her a tall glass of cool water. She smiled softly and stepped into his hug. 'And you take care of me, too, Kabir.'

'Not as much as I should have these last few years,' he said, giving me a sad smile over the top of her head.

'Nonsense,' she said, pulling back to kiss him lightly on the lips.

Feeling slightly like a voyeur, I watched the two banter. It was so encouraging to see Kabir back to his old self; to see the two interacting so intimately, almost like newlyweds. With little Jianna, they were the sweetest family, taking care of each other, leaning on each other when circumstances demanded.

Love will always push past adversity, and triumph, I mused.

I thought about Vivaan and what he said about going to Rajgad Fort. He didn't even tell me, but even if he had, would I have really paid attention to the significance of that day for him? I'd been so wrapped up in my own misery of losing the book deal that I was barely giving time to his hurting the last few weeks. I knew that the drugs weren't his, but in all the time and effort he took to make sure I had absolutely believed him... did I put that same time and effort into convincing him that I *did* trust him?

I didn't know, my mind said. But in my heart, I knew the answer was no. I was so upset with what had happened to me that I didn't take the time to show him that I still trusted him. That I still believed in him, my Vivaan.

Why was I sitting in here, when I should have been with him? If the roles were reversed, how would I feel sitting on a beautiful beach by myself, while he was holed up in a villa working? I was sure I would have told him I understood, and part of me probably would. But I was also convinced that, deep down, I would have been hurt. Was that how he felt?

Some things only happen for the briefest moment, like a raindrop. You can catch it and hold it close, but if you don't reach out to capture that drop of water, you lose it forever. I needed to capture this moment and find Vivaan.

I closed my journal and went upstairs to freshen up. I put on some fresh clothing and pulled my hair up. Then, gazing at the person in front of me in the mirror, I put on makeup with more care than I had in a long time. One thing I had learned: don't ever stop trying to impress the one you love.

Going back downstairs, I was glad to see Kabir and Nisha still there, although they were so wrapped up with each other that I had to cough to get their attention. 'Can you point me in the direction to where Vivaan is on the beach?' I asked.

By then, the two of them had settled onto the soft leather couch. Nisha's legs were tucked across Kabir's lap and they were whispering. I waited for a second and realised they hadn't even heard me. 'Nisha!' I said loudly and giggled a little when the two jumped like two schoolkids caught in a forbidden embrace.

They both turned to me, blushing in the soft afternoon sunlight. 'Did you need something?' Nisha asked absently.

'Can you tell me where Vivaan is?'

Nisha, her attention broken by Kabir's nuzzling, gave me directions. I had no idea if she even knew her left from her right at that point, she was so distracted. But Kabir didn't seem to find any fault with her instructions. Of course, I thought to myself as I slipped on my shoes to walk to the beach, he probably didn't know up from down by then either.

'We'll be gone for *several hours*,' I said pointedly, and softly closed the door behind me, leaving the revitalised couple in peace. I didn't think they heard me leave.

I was actually quite surprised to find Vivaan as easily as I did, given that Baga Beach was a very crowded destination. In fact, when I first stepped on the sand and slipped my shoes off, I looked around, disoriented by the throngs of people.

But of course, he had been my true north for a very long time; all I had to do was think about him and our paths managed to cross, even on a heavily populated beach. And there he was, stretched out on a large towel under the umbrella Nisha had set up to protect Kabir's delicate skin. He seemed asleep as I approached but when I was only a few steps away, he opened his eyes, looked directly at me, and smiled.

I reached out for his steadying hand as I sat down beside him and snuggled my hip against his. Instinctively, our arms went around each other's waists. We fit so perfectly together. Falling in love means opening yourself up to someone else. It is as natural as breathing.

I laid my head on his shoulder, smelling the salt and the sun on his skin. His arm ran up and down mine and I loved feeling his strong hand caressing me. It felt so right.

Love is the healing force in the world, and one cannot discount its power. It defines us. It changes us. We just have to allow it to happen.

I felt Vivaan's shoulder drop a little bit and I looked up, just as he was dipping his head down to brush his lips against mine. As we kissed, I felt his pain, but I also felt his love.

There is only one person for everyone. That is the person that you want to laugh with, to cry with. They make scents smell sweeter, flavours dance on our tongues, and melodies in the dullest sounds. This is the one person who you want to bare your soul to, opening doors that are locked up tight to every other person in the world. You can see your life reflected in their eyes, and it is so amazing, you never want to close your own eyes. This person makes the most insignificant moments into celebrations just with a kind word, a phone call during a stressful day, or a simple hug. The words 'I love you' are no longer three flat, almost meaningless words, but a constant festival to mark your days together. I had met that person, and that person was sitting right beside me.

We talked about everything and nothing. No subject was too much or not enough. At that moment it was just us. Together. Nothing else mattered.

We talked for hours about everything, my writing, his company, our early months together. When we got tired of sitting, he pulled me to my feet and we walked down the beach, our hands laced tightly together. We smiled at the dogs stretched out on the warm sand, and then laughed as a cow wandered on to the sand, soon to be joined by a small herd. People watched them, but nobody seemed to be annoyed by seeing the large mammals on the sand.

Regret isn't in what we say but in what remains unsaid.

'Can I tell you something?' I started tentatively, not wanting to bring back the darkness in Vivaan's eyes, but desperately wanted to address what he considered the failure of his company.

For a second, I did see the shadows return, but they dissipated quickly as he gave me a magnificent smile. 'You haven't been saying enough?' he teased. 'I thought we've been talking all afternoon.'

I gave him a smile back and took a deep breath. 'It's about your company, Vivaan. I know it has been tremendously unfair and very hard on you, but I don't see it as the end. You can run and hide from a problem, but its proximity doesn't make it go away.'

He hummed a little. 'I don't know if it is or not, Meera. When I lost the company, I felt like something was ripped out of my heart. I've been feeling like such a failure. No. A victim.'

I looked earnestly in his eyes. 'Don't consider yourself a victim. Someone took advantage of you and that cost you a lot, but it didn't cost you everything. What happened challenged you. It hurt you and damaged your reputation. But you cannot give up. Your hopes and dreams may have departed from the path you expected, but they have not been denied to you.'

'You don't think so?'

'I don't. We need to hold on to our hopes and dreams because if we loosen our grip, they seem to take wing, but will crash to the earth if we allow them to.'

'They did crash, though,' he said.

'Destiny doesn't make life happen one way just because we demand it to be so. When life is in pieces, we have to take those pieces to build something new.'

'Do you really think so?'

'I do. We are given challenges but we are also given

hope. Bad things can happen quickly, but amazing things can happen just as quickly. Today, our book of life is open to a sad passage, but the page will turn and our book will become happy once more.'

'I hope you're right,' he said. I watched him smile and then frown once more.

'What are you thinking about, Vivaan?'

'The person who did this to me. To us. I don't know what I would ever do if I saw him again.'

'Forgiving someone is reaching into the fire. There will be pain, at first, but then you start to heal and live again,' I said. 'We think it is okay to be angry at another person, but that hatred is an acid, eroding at our very soul. But you have to forgive yourself first, if you fail at something, or didn't do something you should have done but kept putting it off. When you forgive yourself, you can truly move on.'

'I worked so hard to start Musafir, though,' he said angrily. 'Even time can't buff out some memories. But I have to admit, I have been feeling sorry for myself.'

I responded gently. 'Self-pity is such a destructive emotion, Vivaan. If you need to, give in to it, but only give it power for a few minutes. Then lock it back up and move on with your life. You can't live if you are mired down by this emotion, and what a waste that would be. Nobody wants to struggle, Vivaan, but those challenges bring with them the gift of living. Give in to the pain, let it convey its lesson, and then ask it to leave.'

'I hate pain,' he grumbled.

'The hurt within you can be pushed away, but—like water—it is going to seep back into your heart. You need to let it fill you sometimes, so you can use it to rise to the top once more.'

He grinned and cupped my cheek with his hand. 'You are a wise woman.'

He moved to kiss me, but I had more to say. 'There, in your face, I can see pain and sadness. But I also see threads of hope in your eyes and I know they will grow stronger.'

'How can life make me feel so fragmented while I also feel so unbroken?'

'Because life does that sometimes,' I whispered. 'There is a time for everything. A time for pain, yes, but also a time to heal. We can't change who we were, but we can change who we are.'

'You love me,' he said simply.

'I do. And so, I feel you. Love means truly feeling the same hurt that someone else feels. But it also means sharing their happiness as intimately as if it came from you. We will be happy again, Vivaan.'

As the bright sun slipped into its orange evening cloak and started its evening trek toward the horizon, we wandered to one of the restaurants beckoning customers with lively music. I texted Nisha to let her know we would be dining out; she texted back that they were doing the same.

'Do you think Pari will mind?' I asked her.

'Pari's thrilled,' she texted back. 'She's watching Jianna!'

Well, that settled it. Vivaan and I relaxed with our beverages and anxiously awaited our food, which turned out to be a delicious version of Navratan Korma. I'm pretty sure I hummed happily throughout the entire meal. Maybe it was the salty air, maybe it was the different food, but I'm pretty sure my satiated feeling was because Vivaan and I were once more in sync with each other.

After dinner, we left the colourful lights of the beachside restaurant, following the darkness back to the mumbling surf, whispering its secrets just beyond our vision. In the cooling night air, we walked back up the beach, following shadowed landmarks until we reached our abandoned umbrella. Silently, not wanting to break the magic, we gathered our belongings.

We headed back to the villa and I was content, knowing we were both literally and figuratively walking the same path together once more.

And from now on, we would take each step to our future hand in hand.

23
FATE

Wow, so they really think they can fight me? You know, sometimes, being able to see what all four are thinking is as annoying as listening to a song played off-key.

I'm not sure how this happened. I was supposed to crush them with adversity. My plan was to liven things up by making them fight for their happiness ... and fail.

Instead, here they are, trekking off to Goa and starting to piece things back together. I really thought I pushed them down much, much harder. These four are tough, I guess. Much tougher than I imagined. Of course, we are only talking about emotional movements so far. So maybe, even though they think they have the worst of everything behind them, in reality, peace of mind is not as important as they believe it is.

They still have so many things to work through.

We have to see how Vivaan is going to pull off a career. Even if he doesn't have Musafir, he still has to make a living. He can't live on love, after all. I'm sure he's going to do something, but will it ever be on the grand scheme that he had planned? I doubt it.

I am enjoying watching Meera struggling with her writing. She had it too easy before, her first books came without much of a struggle. Maybe she is just going to have to give up on her writing too. It certainly seems like hope is trickling through her fingers.

It's fun watching her toss and turn at night, eyes opening wide as she tries to figure out how to make her book move forward. Because that car has most certainly run out of petrol. I think she better start thinking about a career for herself. Maybe she can work for Vivaan... oh, wait! He doesn't have a business anymore! Ha ha!

And then, there are Kabir and Nisha. In her inspired attempt to reunite everyone with their dreams, she pretty much sapped the rest of their savings. We all know how bitter couples can grow when they are fighting about money. I hear that that is one of the top causes of divorce.

It's looking like this trip to Goa might just blow up in Nisha's face.

They are fools, total fools.

Just because you expect something to work out one way doesn't mean it will. That is what puts the spice in life though. And I am much stronger than them.

I am the bird that flies through the storm. Why? Because I can. I have the strength to pull my wings through the winds and the rain, weaving in and out of warm and cold drafts.

You can try to keep up with me; you can push yourself to fly through your own storm. Just be careful you don't smack into a wall while you're dancing on the breeze. Hitting things when you're travelling at a high speed... well, it isn't very forgiving.

24

VIVAAN

Our amazing three days in Goa were about to end. Tonight was our last evening in this amazing beach community ... at least for now.

I woke up early and slipped out of the villa, wanting to take an early morning walk in the community and maybe head to the bustling Mapusa Market, hopefully before it became too busy. I wanted to pick up a gift for Pari to thank her for opening up her home to us.

As much as I enjoyed the sand and surf, I also loved walking through Goa's neighbourhoods, taking in every nuance of the town. After visiting Braganza House with Meera and Pari yesterday, I began to see subtler Portuguese influences peppered throughout the town, from a colourful tile pattern to distinct arrangements within the lush gardens in the area.

While walking, I let my thoughts drift over our entire trip to Goa, one that was truly a brilliant decision on Nisha's part. Usually the quieter of the couple, Nisha's gentle mind inserted the practical aspect into Kabir's dreams. It was uncharacteristic of her to make such a bold move like arranging this trip, but in typical Nisha fashion, it was well-thought out and I was touched to think that while she could have limited the trip to her family, she extended it to include Meera and me.

I learned several things over the last few days. Watching Nisha and Kabir's love rejuvenate, much like mine and Meera's seemed to have, I realised how quickly two people could be separated by adversity. Even challenges thought to be positive, such as Kabir launching Kafe Kabir, could turn negative if people didn't respect and take the time to care for the people around them while following their dreams.

Ironically, despite my travels often taking me away from Meera, we had managed to stay close. Until I lost my startup with the drug fiasco. Then, when I was forced to stay home and was physically closer to Meera, we seemed to start to drift apart, because her focus was on losing her book deal and mine was on losing my company. Instead of turning to each other for support, we turned into ourselves.

We were all fortunate for this trip to help us refocus and reprioritise. I was most thankful for Meera and the talking-to she gave me the other day. It was as if she collected the pieces of myself that I lost and fused them back together, bringing them home to my soul.

The crowds were beginning to thicken, and I realised I was nearing the famous Mapusa Market. I smiled, already looking forward to the crush of bodies and loud voices.

It was a fun trip, and I enjoyed squeezing my way around people to barter with vendors for trinkets. I had learned during our stay how much Pari enjoyed sewing her own clothes, so I was especially happy to find a cloth vendor and hastily started to barter for a beautiful print for her.

I was delighted at the price we settled on eventually, although I feigned disgust, to the seller's obvious enjoyment. Package in hand, I turned to hurry away before he could tempt me with more of his wares.

'Vivaan?' I heard a voice call across the heads of several people. I spun around, looking for a familiar face but saw no one. 'Vivaan,' the man called again, and I stopped to wait for the person to emerge from the crowds.

As soon as I got a good look at his face, I was astounded. 'Parth!' I said, greeting the man I had shared an Uber with in Bangalore. 'What are you doing here, my friend? How are you?'

He laughed; a deep, hearty sound. 'I'm here to celebrate my birthday with some friends,' he responded. 'And to answer your other question, I am terrific—much, much better than when you and I last saw each other!'

I was surprised. The last time we spoke, he was a pleasant companion, but it was obvious that he was a thoroughly unhappy man who felt trapped in a boring, dead-end job. I knew the feeling well from when I worked at the bank. But now, a different man stood in front of me, eyes shining brightly. His smile lit up his face and his voice had an excited lift.

'Do you need to be anywhere soon?' he continued. 'I would love to catch up with you over a coffee. So much has happened over the last few months!'

'I would love to,' I responded, curious at the complete change in his attitude. In fact, I don't need to be anywhere for a few hours.

We looked around for a place to sit but decided to walk around a block where the crowds were thinner, and we could speak without having to raise our voices. Sitting in a café that reminded me nostalgically of Kafe Kabir, I spoke first. 'Now, tell me what has changed in your world. You look like a completely different man! What is your secret to happiness?'

Parth laughed again. 'It's no secret, but yes, everything has changed.' He leaned forward conspiratorially and looked me in the eye. 'I took your advice,' he said in an exaggerated whisper.

'You did?' I responded, delighted. 'You left your company?'

'Yes!' he said so enthusiastically that other people turned around to stare at his outburst. Amused, I watched him give an apologetic smile with a shrug that showed the perfect balance of regret without embarrassment.

I took a sip of my latte. The rich, creamy beverage was delicious, but it lacked the depth that I got from Kafe Kabir. Wow, I really was becoming a coffee snob. 'Thank you for this,' I said and lifted the mug in a silent toast. 'To you and your next steps...' I offered. 'So, what are you doing now?'

Parth took a sip of his own coffee thoughtfully. 'Well, it's this. Have you ever sat down with a senior and listened to the stories that they have to share about the 'good old days'? Maybe it's a story about how your grandparents met; maybe it's their childhood memories. You know, back before television was even a household item.'

I nodded. 'Absolutely. My Auntie used to tell the most amazing stories.'

'Can you recall them now?' he asked curiously.

I frowned. 'Bits and pieces, but nothing specific unfortunately. And Auntie passed away about a year ago.' Just thinking of the night I received the phone call brought a wave of sadness over me.

Parth winced a little. 'I'm sorry for your loss,' he said sombrely.

I shrugged and gestured for him to continue. I had a feeling I was going to love what my friend had to say.

He sat back and collected his thoughts once more. 'The same thing happened to our family, but before my grandfather passed away, one of my younger cousins 'interviewed' him for a school project and happened to record the conversation. Now, back to your aunt's stories. Imagine how precious that would be to you now, to have her own words at your fingertips so you could remember them over and over again.'

'Like a memoir?' I asked.

He nodded. 'Yes and no. Yes, in that they are her stories in her words. But no in the sense that it is not necessarily a formalised piece of writing that you can order from your bookstore.'

'Keep going,' I said. 'I think I'm liking this idea a lot.'

'My company is called 'Yaadein'.' He stopped to see if I understood the significance of the name.

"Memories',' I said, deep in thought. 'A beautiful name. But what do you do?'

'My staff, when it is up and running, will manage a group of freelance interviewers across India. At the request of a senior, or the family, we can go and conduct a series of interviews with the person. The interviews will be recorded, of course.'

'It sounds expensive,' I mused.

He shook his head. 'That's the beauty of this. The way I have everything set up, it's a tiered system. For a small price, the recordings will be transcribed and given to the family. For a different price, they can have the recordings. For a larger investment, we will have staff writers at Yaadein develop a formal mini-memoir, with a book cover, and get it professionally printed. With the publishing platforms available these days, they can order one book, or one hundred!'

'What about combining a number of interviews from members of the same family?' I suggested.

Parth's eyes lit up. 'That could be the platinum programme,' he said. 'What a great idea.'

'It's a fantastic idea,' I responded. 'It will capture all those stories, family history that might otherwise be lost when a family member passes away.'

'In this world of smartphones and smart devices, we are looking at the future,' he said, 'at the price of forgetting the past. When my grandfather died, my cousin remembered he had those recordings and he brought them to the funeral celebration. It was only ten minutes of recordings, but to hear his voice, to feel his laughter rumble through the room … it was a priceless gift we will have always.'

'I do love it,' I said, with sincere respect for my clever friend. 'So, have you launched it?'

'We're close to launching right now,' he said. 'We'll be starting small, but it has the potential to grow tremendously as the idea takes hold.'

I took another sip. 'I am sure you will be very successful, Parth. I am very happy with what you have accomplished in the months since we met!'

'I truly wouldn't have had the courage to do anything like this, had I not met you, Vivaan. For that, I am so grateful that destiny put us in that car the same day.' He clapped his hands happily. 'Now you! Tell me what has been going on with you since we met?'

I was hesitant to mention anything about the events that had unfolded in my life, not wanting my frustration and shame to taint Parth's excitement. After all, I was the one who convinced him to take a chance ... what a fool I would seem now that he followed my advice and was soaring, while I had fallen flat on my face.

My fingers worried the edge of the white napkin my coffee cup was sitting on. 'It's nothing as exciting, I'm afraid.'

'But you were going to speak to some investors about your travel company,' he said. 'What happened? Did you change your mind about starting your company?'

I shook my head sadly. 'No, I did manage to start it, even though the investors decided not to take on my startup,' I told him the whole story about how I was building the company and was on our first trip when the police found drugs in my bag.

'Oh no,' he groaned. 'Was it the person who was sitting beside you?'

'It had to have been,' I said. 'Because I can assure you, they were not mine!'

'I can tell,' Parth said sincerely. 'You would never put your company in jeopardy like that, I know.'

I starred out the window for a few long moments, feeling the frustration and shame once more. 'Never,' I said vehemently. 'But it doesn't matter. The accusation was made, and enough doubt was cast over me. The company folded almost right after it started.'

'I can't believe it.'

'Honestly, I still can't either. All my hopes and dreams. Gone.'

'It is very odd hearing these words from the man who had given me so much hope. But I think you're going to be able to regain it. In fact, it's easy when you think of it this way. Your success or failure is yours to own. You are the weaver of your destiny, whether it happens because you made a mistake, or if someone wronged you. Of if they supported you. Success and failure are merely signposts, the roads are yours.'

'I don't know about that. I used to see the future so clearly but I can't now. Once, I felt like I was sitting under the most brilliant star, one that guided me and brought good fortune to my life. But you know what happens with stars? They can be there one moment and come crashing to earth the next.'

'No, my friend. I do not believe that' Parth said. 'It's all about how you live your life, not what seems to be lighting your way. The story of life can be summarised in a few short words. It is never-ending. No matter what you are going through, no matter how difficult the journey is, no matter how fate tests us, life never stops; it endures.'

I ran my fingers through my hair, feeling that old frustration. 'I just don't understand though. How did this happen?'

'A simple question may end up taking years to form. And

decades to solve. And sometimes, there is no cause for this effect. Not really,' he said sadly. 'But don't wait for time to take away the pain. Take control and do it yourself.'

'How?'

'I'm not sure but I do know this. You need to believe one truth about yourself, Vivaan: you are more qualified than you realise and more gifted than you can believe at this moment. Take your talents and fly. Hope is the catalyst that gets things done.'

His enthusiasm was contagious and I grinned a little bit. 'But there were so many attacks, not just on me, but Meera too.' I told him how this whole incident affected Meera's career and life.

'How can you judge a person's life by a few actions or the people that they influenced? Maybe judgment can't and shouldn't be made on anybody's life but your own. Vivaan, life is like a puddle and sometimes you need to just leave that water alone. The grime eventually settles, leaving clear water. If you keep going back to it, you will only stir the mud up again.'

'Interesting analogy,' I said drily. 'But sometimes I just can't wait. The more time I try to figure out things, the tighter my situation becomes.'

'Time is a busy word, isn't it? Time can fall behind, time can race ahead; it can be on your hands or tell you something. The tragedy, though, is also when time runs out. It most certainly has not run out for you.'

'You do have a point.'

'Of course I do,' he chuckled. 'So, what will you do now?'

'I'm not sure,' I confessed. 'I'll need to—'

'Wait!' he cried. 'I have an idea!'

Well, this was unexpected. I felt an absurd glow of hope in my stomach while I waited for Parth's next words. 'Tell me,' I urged.

'I need a CFO,' he said. 'I feel that Yaadein is going to be a huge success. So many people are asking when we'll be ready. But while I am hiring the freelancers I need, I can barely keep track of everything now. I need someone who I can trust to be my right-hand man, someone to handle all the financial aspects while I throw myself into marketing the company.'

I thought about his idea. It was an interesting one, but did I truly want to go back into the bland world of finance? After all, it was the black-and-white bleakness of those numbers and incessant calculations that drove me half-crazy in the first place.

'Hm, I don't know...' I started and took the last gulp of my now-cold latte to give myself a chance to think. Yuck.

'The more I think about it, the more I love the idea,' Parth enthused, leaning across the table. 'I can tell what you're thinking: crunching numbers. That's what you wanted to get away from, right?'

I nodded.

'I can offer you a very good package and stock options,' he said. 'You'll be coming in at the ground level, helping me to get things up and running. You'll be my number one guy.'

'Parth, this is a truly generous offer,' I started.

Our coffee empty, we stood up and left the café together, stepping back into the bright sun. 'First of all,' he continued, 'it is not too generous if that is what you are thinking. I really need a man I can trust, because I am not a numbers person. Second, I cannot tell you how grateful I am for your words of inspiration that day. If it wasn't for you, honestly Vivaan, I would still be in my miserable job doing my miserable work.

'It was you, and you alone, who gave me the confidence to leave and start my own company. For that, I cannot thank you enough.' He stopped and looked at the time on his phone. 'I'm sorry but I need to run now... my friends have likely slept off last night's festivities and will be looking for the birthday boy.'

I laughed. 'It was great to see you again,' I said. We pulled out our phones and exchanged numbers this time.

'Vivaan,' he said. 'Take your time in thinking this over. I know it's a big step, but I think you and I will work well together. Of course, you'll have to come to Bangalore, but'—he held out his arms jokingly—'I am a fun person to work with! It won't be a bore, I promise.'

'I really appreciate the offer,' I responded sincerely. 'I will definitely give it a lot of thought and be in touch as soon as I decide, if that's okay?'

'Of course!' Parth's phone started to ring, and he looked at the caller ID, rolling his eyes. 'And there they are,' he laughed. 'I'll talk to you soon!'

With a few footsteps, he disappeared into the crowd so suddenly that I wondered for a brief moment if I had imaged the encounter.

I thought about Parth's news as I made my way back to the villa. That night, the four of us took Pari out to a restaurant to thank her for taking us in. We laughed and had a great time, and I gave her my humble gift. She was delighted at the gesture and invited us to return anytime.

Pari then turned her wise eyes to mine. 'You are responsible for your life, not Kabir's, not Meera's, and not mine. Yours. Just as I am not responsible for yours. The only one who can live that life is you. Go live it, my friend.' Then she looked at the group. 'You only have one shot at living this life. Live it with passion, not regrets.'

I hugged her, my throat tight at her offer. Between her confidence in me, and learning about Parth's career change, I was filled with bright hope. Before we left for Goa, I felt like I was on an island, trying to cross a long channel to get back to the land I knew would bring me happiness. I could see it, I knew it was there, but how could I navigate those dangerous waters to get back to where I wanted to be? Somehow in a matter of days, a bridge had been built, but though the journey would still be long, I knew I could make my way back.

Arriving at my apartment that night, I felt the relief of coming home again. After being in Pari's immaculate villa for so many days, I noticed that things were a little untidy. But still, it was good to be home. As much as I loved travelling, it was always a relief to be back in my own space again.

After tossing my laundry into the hamper, I took some time to wander around the rooms that made me feel so welcome; it was as if I was greeting an old friend once more. Finally, I felt settled down, sliding into my recliner and flipping open my laptop.

I wanted to do a little research into Parth's idea. Always a numbers guy, I was curious to learn the statistics of the elderly in Bangalore, and then I wondered about Pune. I started clicking through links to different regions in India and felt that familiar ache that grew from wanting to share the beauty of our country with other people.

Exiting my web browser, my screen flashed to my desktop and I saw one of the many pictures I had taken of the Hirni Waterfalls in Jharkhand. Suddenly, I was there once more, looking up at the cascading falls, hearing the rush of water echoing in my ears, and feeling a light mist on my face. I loved how the Ramgarha River spread tendrils of plummeting liquid down the rocks until it settled calmly into its next journey.

How tall were the falls? I frowned, trying to remember, and turned my browser back on to look up more information about Hirni Falls. I ended up on an Instagram feed and tears filled my eyes as I looked at the beautiful images of our country.

Meera called later that evening and I was quaking with excitement. 'I've made a couple of decisions that I was going to tell you about,' I announced.

She could hear the enthusiasm in my voice and her tone matched mine when she responded. 'Tell me!'

'A couple of things,' I started, still staring at the picture on my desktop. 'First, I decided I'm going to take the job that Parth offered, assuming it's still available.'

'I think that's a very wise decision,' Meera responded. 'I know finance isn't something you're eager to get back into, but his company sounds like a great idea. I have no doubt there will be a lot of challenges, but I have a feeling you will enjoy working with him.'

'I'm sure I will,' I said. 'I wish you had had a chance to meet him, but... ahem... you were sleeping in.' I couldn't help teasing her about her lazy morning the day I went to the market, remembering returning to the villa only moments after she admitted to waking up.

'It was a lazy day,' she protested lightly.

'You know I'm teasing, right?' I took her giggle over the phone to be a 'yes'. I continued. 'I'll call Parth tomorrow to get more details, but I do think it is a good next step for me. Plus, he knows it's a stepping stone for me so when I am able to, I'll return to my own dream of taking tour groups on trips. Which brings me to my other decision.'

'You are full of surprises tonight, Vivaan.' Now it was her turn to tease.

'I am,' I returned. 'I've decided that I'm going to start blogging about some of my trips and share my photos on Instagram.'

'What a great idea!' she said. 'Your photos are amazing.'

'I can't wait to take you to some of these places myself.' And suddenly, I was aware that I didn't feel the pang I had been feeling when I thought of travelling. When I lost

Musafir, I felt like my gateway to travel had been closed. The thought of travelling, I realised now, felt like an impossible dream then.

But I knew I could turn my back on my regrets now. I didn't need to keep them in the present.

I could start to inch that gate back open, and I knew I would be able to travel again. Until that happened, I could quench that hunger by sharing my adventures on a blog. Who knew? That could attract even more attention, so by the time I was able to start my company again, I could have a social media following.

'Do you think you can help me set up those accounts?' I asked Meera. We agreed to meet the next morning, so she could help me with that process.

I crawled into my bed that night. As I looked up at the ceiling, I felt happy that things were starting to turn around for me again. This time, as I made my way back to my dreams, I would make sure my friends were able to rediscover their dreams too.

But I knew that wouldn't be the end of the story. It isn't enough just to achieve your dreams and expect them to stay right in place. They need to be nurtured through hard work. And they might not always fit together, but our job was to figure out how to fit them together. I knew we would.

25
KABIR

Nisha and I shared a beautiful, warm embrace before we left for our walk. Since our trip to Goa, we had grown even closer than I could have imagined. Sometimes she and Jianna joined me on my walks; sometimes I went alone. This day, she was wide awake and babbling happily so we left for a walk before the predicted rain came in that night.

I was feeling better than I had in a long time. My scars had healed to the point that the pain had dulled from discomfort to barely a memory anymore. I was thankful that Nisha and our friends had taken such good care of me during the early stages of the healing process, taking up the reins that my amazing doctors and surgeons had initiated in their excellent care.

Don't push people away, but remember that keeping them near to you is not enough. You must also allow them into your soul by sharing your hopes and dreams with them. I did that with Nisha, every day now.

Of the utmost importance, Nisha and I agreed, were my daily walks, now that I was able to venture out without worrying about the bright Indian sun hurting my body. The walks were critical, not just to bring my body back to the level of fitness that I enjoyed, but also to help clear my mind of all the clutter that formed when I worried about finances and mourned the loss of my beloved café.

I knew I would rebuild, but as Nisha and I pored over figures, we had no idea how it would happen. The savings that she had were sustaining us, but would not support us indefinitely. Nisha talked about going to work somewhere, and I would have supported it, but I knew her heart was in raising Jianna. Our little girl was heartily into her third year, and every day was a new discovery ... and a new challenge. Nisha didn't want to miss a moment, and I was thankful that my wife was content to stay at home.

All these things passed through my mind as we made our way past colourful storefronts, crossing busy streets. As usual, I didn't know where we would be walking; like Jianna, who delighted in the smallest things in our world, each day was a new discovery.

And then we saw the white double archways welcoming people to the Savitribai Phule Pune University. I loved walking in all the university campuses, taking in the different students and the cross-sections of emotions: frustration, excitement, anxiousness ... whatever their education handed them that day.

This university, in particular, was a favourite destination of mine. There was something invigorating about wandering through the smartly maintained gardens, but I was particularly drawn to a pathway enveloped by dark, thoughtful, and old trees. Walking down that path felt like walking into a secret. A delightful secret, one kept close to the heart.

After making our way through the walkway, ducking carefully under some of the trees that were encroaching further, we returned to one of the green gardens and sat happily on one of the benches.

A group of young students made their way past us and we nodded our hellos to them before my eyelids slid shut and I turned my face to the warm sunlight.

'Excuse me,' I heard tentatively.

I opened my eyes and the group of students had backtracked, now standing in front of our family. 'Yes, can I help you?' I asked, curious.

'You aren't from Kafe Kabir by any chance, are you?' the young girl asked.

My face widened into a wide grin. 'I am,' I confirmed. 'I am... was... the owner, Kabir.' I reached out my hand and shook her hand.

'Oh wow,' she said before turning to one of her friends. 'I told you it was him.' Suddenly, the entire group was murmuring, some in greeting, some in surprise as they realised who I was. The girl dropped on to the bench beside me, her face sad. 'I was so very sorry to hear about the fire.'

I pursed my lips, touched by her sincere look. 'Thank you,' I stammered. 'I appreciate that. I take it you had been to Kafe Kabir?'

Several people in the group nodded. 'I didn't get there as often as I wanted to, but I loved going there,' she said.

I glanced at Nisha. She was grinning, enjoying the conversation we were having

A young man cleared his throat. 'I remember going there one time and didn't realise I was short on funds. By the time I realised it, you had already poured my coffee and gave it to me anyway. You didn't have to ... and a lot of people wouldn't have ... but you were very kind and told me it was payment enough to promise to go back and study hard.'

'And have you?' I cocked my eyebrow at him teasingly.

'Yes sir,' he confirmed. 'That very day I was studying for an exam. It was one of the highest marks I've gotten.'

'That is terrific,' Nisha said, nodding her approval.

'Then it was worth the investment,' I winked.

He laughed, and then sobered. 'I was thinking about that the day we heard about the fire. And you were hurt?' he asked gently.

I nodded but deliberately brightened up. 'I am much better now, though,' I said.

'Oh good!' another person in the group chimed in. 'So you will be rebuilding soon?'

I sighed. 'If only it were that easy,' I said. 'It takes money to rebuild.'

They groaned collectively, all sympathising with the frustrations of being financially limited. 'That's too bad,' the first girl said. 'I really, really miss your coffee.'

Collectively, the group murmured again, and several chimed in with stories of local coffee disappointments. 'It's just not the same,' one person said sadly. 'The cafeteria coffee is horrible.'

'What about coffee stalls?' Nisha asked, curiously. 'Didn't I see one close to the edge of the campus?'

'One,' somebody confirmed. 'And I guess it's not bad. But it's not Kafe Kabir's coffee.'

'No...' another piped up.

We talked coffee beans for a little longer and the baby delighted them with her cooing.

I asked them their names. 'When Kafe Kabir opens again... and I know it will somehow... I want you all to visit. I've enjoyed chatting with you all and I would love to buy you a coffee.' I looked at the boy who had run short on money that day. 'And a second one for you,' I teased.

The skies were starting to thicken with clouds and I remembered the weather forecast. We were still quite a way from home and I wanted to get back before the rain started. Nisha and I stood up, shook everybody's hands in farewell and headed home.

Your perception of events reflects the outcome. Even the simplest event can become the most meaningful when we assign our perceptions.

We walked in silence. I was thinking about the group of students, all eager to tell me their coffee woes.

Just as a thought began to form in my mind, Nisha cleared

her throat. I knew she was preparing to say something important when she did that.

'Those kids sure missed your coffee,' she commented.

'I know,' I said, 'but they're going to have to wait a little longer. We aren't in a position to rebuild yet.'

'About that,' she mused. 'Maybe we could rebuild Kafe Kabir earlier than planned ... and bring it closer to them.'

'How do you mean?' I started to ask, but our conversation was halted. The rain started and we dashed the final half block to home.

We were laughing but out of breath from jogging the path to our apartment after the deluge started. Instead of cursing the rain as I might have done in the past, the cold sogginess only made me laugh harder.

'You should have brought a raincoat like we did,' Nisha said when we walked into our apartment and she took off her jacket. 'You're soaking wet!'

I couldn't help it. I picked her up and swung her around, making her half shriek, half giggle. 'And now you're as wet as I am,' I responded, and shook my mane of black hair in her direction.

'What has gotten into you?' she clucked, pulling at her damp, thin shirt before she grabbed a kitchen towel and tossed it to me. She then proceeded to take the baby's wet jacket off.

I caught the towel deftly and started to dry my hair. But then, I looked down at Jianna, who was staring up at me with a tentative smile and curious eyes. I bent down in front of her and shook my head again. She squealed happily when several large drops landed on her, too.

I jogged into the bedroom and changed my clothes quickly, then came out and scooped her up. She ran her fingers through my wet hair and then in her dry locks; apparently, she wasn't done with the 'Daddy's all wet' game.

After we settled in, Nisha sat close to me on the sofa, her eyes dancing.

'I have an idea,' she started excitedly. 'I was thinking about those kids back at the university. What if we started a coffee stall instead of building a full-blown café?'

'What?' I said. 'Do you think we could?'

'It would be a much smaller investment and it sounds like you'd have some steady customers.'

'Hmmmm. I like the idea, but it is very different from what I was doing at Kafe Kabir.'

'Well, different but the same. Kind of like life. What we consider our future is only our perception of that future. When we realise this, we take the power away from destiny and reclaim it for ourselves. And just as we take the power away from the future, we should not be giving it to the past either. Take it, examine it, and then set it aside. But past or present, use it to make yourself better, always.'

'Wow,' I breathed. 'You are so insightful, my beautiful wife.'

She waved her hand in dismissal but grinned. 'After all, coffee is coffee. Let me clarify... Kabir's coffee is Kabir's coffee. You can go back to your old suppliers and of course, you still have all the recipes. We just need some equipment and would only need a little area to open the business. What do you think?'

I drummed my fingers on the table, deep in thought. 'It certainly is a different image than the one you cultivated when we owned the café,' she said slowly and I could see some doubt creeping in. 'Maybe it wouldn't work. What if you don't like it?'

But I loved the idea.

I understood her hesitation, knowing how proud I was to be spearheading Kafe Kabir. This would be a much smaller scale. Takeout only, no place for people to sit. 'I'm not as worried about my image right now as you would think. It seems like it would be a step down perhaps, but Nisha, I have missed the customers so much. I've missed frothing the milk and watching their delighted faces when they took their first sip of my coffee.'

Nisha, my steadfast supporter, nodded firmly. 'Then I think we need to figure out how to make this work, Kabir. We can't succeed until we force it to happen.'

I let out a breath I didn't realise I had been holding. It seemed like such a perfect solution, but without Nisha's understanding and encouragement, I was absolutely nothing.

I reached out and held her hand. 'I guess at the end of the day, it doesn't matter how large or small your coffee shop is,' she said. 'I know it's something that you love doing and I will support you one hundred per cent.'

26

MEERA

I was nervous. I didn't remember the last time I had felt that fluttering nervousness, the fight-or-flight desire ... that at the moment was strongly suggesting that I choose flight. I scrambled off the wooden bench where I had been sitting and pretended to inspect the posters on the bulletin board.

'Help wanted in the library ... weekend hours preferred.'

'Roommate needed. Must be a non-smoker and willing to help with chores.'

'Books for sale. Psychology, sociology, accounting. Like new condition.'

I smiled at that one.

I scrutinised each word on every poster. And then read them again. I resisted taking out my phone to look at the time, knowing that I had arrived almost a half hour before my interview.

Sitting down again, I thought about the events that brought me to this day. I struggled with my new book for several months after returning from Goa. Nothing seemed to be working well for me; the words that had been my constant companions seemed to have ditched me or were hiding, or something. I just wasn't sure.

What I was sure about was my next book just was not coming together. I would manage to pull together a half of a scene before deleting it again. I tried different mediums, writing a hard copy, which I loved the most; I tried working on my laptop. I tried inspirational music, upbeat music, everything. Nothing brought the words out of my mind, whether I wrote in the early morning, or in bed before I fell asleep.

The only bright spot in an otherwise frustrating life was how strong my relationship with Vivaan was growing. We hadn't talked about marriage anymore since that night so many months ago, but I knew it was on his mind, and it was definitely on my mind as well.

Even with him in Bangalore, we were doing fine with a long-distance relationship. I craved talking to him but knew I needed to let him focus on work. Our time was in the evenings, and we carved out an hour every evening to 'be' together, even if it was only on the phone.

His work with Parth was going very well and, despite his apprehension about going back to the world of numbers, he seemed to be enjoying this type of work tremendously. Between that and the attention his blog had been getting lately, he was much more content than I would have imagined after his dream to start Musafir had been stepped on so cruelly.

I wished I was feeling as contented as he was, I thought dryly to myself.

The same words that were my friends had been waging a war against me. But, like a failed coup, I would turn them back to my side.

I was making changes. About few week ago, I was staring at the walls in my house, desperately trying to find some inspiration somewhere. It occurred to me that one of the reasons I was struggling so much with writing was perhaps because I felt a disconnect with my characters. Which then led to the thought that perhaps I was too isolated from people. After all, when I had written my first two books, a lot of the inspiration was in being at Kafe Kabir, in immersing myself with people.

I needed to be back among people, I determined. But how?

My mind trailed through several possibilities, finally

deciding that a part-time job somewhere would be the most ideal. Something that also used my love for writing.

A few weeks later brought me to my current position, anxiously awaiting for an interview as an English professor.

The rumble of an old door opening indicated that my interview was finally coming to fruition. I introduced myself, and shook the hand of the dean, following him into his office to talk to him about the position he was filling.

'Yes,' I confirmed. 'May I ask why this position is available?'

'It happens sometimes,' he said. 'We had a professor on staff, but she had to leave to take care of a family emergency. I don't know when she'll be back.'

'I understand,' I mused. Although I was trying to temper my excitement, it felt like the job interview was going extraordinarily well. He seemed very pleased with my responses.

The dean nodded so emphatically that his shaggy grey hair shook a bit with the movement. 'I need to be honest with you, Meera. I do have some reservations about why you are interested in the position. After all, you are an author, not a teacher.'

I grinned. 'I find inspiration and stories amid people, so I'm here.'

He gave me a little smile and tented his fingers, putting his elbows on his desk. 'Well, that is interesting.'

'And while it may seem like I'm not qualified—'

'I'd say you are overqualified,' he said.

I shrugged modestly. 'I simply feel that I have a lot to offer your students with my experience and background.'

'You do make a good point.' He nodded, and my heart leaped, suspecting that I would be offered the job very soon.

We spoke for another twenty minutes, and then it happened: the job was mine! I could have hugged him, I was so happy. But I was even more thrilled when he slid open a desk drawer and took out a well-loved copy of my first novel. 'I told my wife that I would be meeting you today,' he said with a blush. 'It would make her entire year if you would be so kind as to autograph it for her?'

That next week was a blur as I scrambled to acquaint myself better with the university system as a whole and transition into this exciting new career move. It might be temporary, but who knew? It certainly seemed like the perfect complement to my writing.

Vivaan flew back to Pune for a quick trip and he came over the morning that was to be my first day at work. His eyes widened as he took in the clothes thrown over the house. 'Did your wardrobe explode?' he teased.

I groaned and slipped into his arms. 'I don't know what to wear,' I moaned. 'Nothing seems right. Should I go traditional or not?'

He pulled back and examined my outfit, taking in my turquoise and gold saree. 'I think you look perfect,' he said endearingly.

'You're biased,' I retorted accusingly before I softened. 'But thank you.'

He started picking up an armful of discarded clothes and I disappeared, re-emerging moments later in a teal outfit. Vivaan grinned at me. 'I don't dare tell you that looks nice too, or you'll go change again, won't you?'

I rolled my eyes, but knew he was probably right … although I was running out of clothes. I started to scurry back around, but Vivaan caught my arm before I could flee again.

'I have a present for you,' he said and held out a small, wrapped box.

Slipping the lid of the box off, I saw a beautiful pen with my name etched on it. It was the match to the pen

I had bought Vivaan the day he launched Musafir. Tears stung my eyes as I lifted the pen out of its box, touched by his thoughtfulness.

'I can't believe you found the exact same pen,' I breathed, loving the weight in my hand.

'It took some time, but I wanted you to have the twin to mine. You and I fit so perfectly together,' he said, his eyes taking on a faraway look before they refocused on mine. 'Now, pack it up. You don't want to be late for your big day!'

I was nowhere near being late for class, but I was happy to arrive early, relieved that the classroom was empty. Flipping on the lights, I sat at the desk and sorted through my notes once again. As the dean of students predicted, my class filled up quickly and I was anxious to meet everyone, hoping I would not disappoint them.

About fifteen minutes before class started, they started drifting in, looking at me curiously. I pushed myself out of my chair and walked around to the other side of the table, taking a casual pose against the desk in hopes to seem more approachable.

I started talking with the students, noting with pleasure how many eager faces were looking at me.

'I am Meera,' I introduced myself nervously. 'I'm an author-turned-professor, and while I don't have the typical background most of your other professors do, I think my experience as a writer will lend a beneficial perspective to you.'

A hand shot up from the back of the class and I nodded to the girl, communicating that she could speak. 'I love your books,' she gushed. 'I was so excited when I heard you would be teaching here!'

A tingle of happiness ran through my body and I gave her a huge grin, which grew even wider as other students murmured similar statements. I didn't just have a full class of eager students; I had a group of faithful readers and fans of my work!

'How did you decide to start writing?' one student asked, leaning forward on her desk.

I smiled. 'I had always wanted to be a writer but I really didn't know where to begin. I used to go to this café a lot and one night, that café hosted an author, who kindled my interest even further. I knew that in order to become a writer, it was as simple as just starting to write. About anything.'

'But you didn't just choose to write about anything,' someone responded, leading me into my next statements.

'No, I developed some friendships with people in the café and as we got to know each other a little better, I realised that they all had fascinating stories of overcoming challenges to achieve their dreams. I was inspired by their history and was driven to capture them in my first book.'

'So it's that simple?'

'For me, in that instance, it was. But writing, just like any other career, is something you have to work at. Ideas come and go, and what seems like a great storyline sometimes just doesn't come to life on a piece of paper the way you expect it to. Just like a child, you can guide it and nurture it, but it will have its own personality and behaviour... influenced by you, definitely, but it is its own entity.'

'You make it sound like a story is a living thing.'

'In a way,' I said thoughtfully, 'it is. You might sit down and start writing with the thought of going in one direction, but sometimes, it is as if your story grows legs and runs off down an entirely different path. In the end, as long as you put your heart and soul into it, it doesn't matter how much the final version changed from your outline.'

'When is your favourite time to write?'

I laughed. 'Just about any time. I love it as my day job but there is something about writing at night too. The night-time minutes travel a different path than those in the day.'

'Do you ever have a hard time describing people? I hear that sometimes, that is the hardest part of writing.'

'Think of it this way,' I suggested. 'Are we actually people, or are we the personification of moments? Perhaps if you look at something a different way, you will be able to pull the words together better. Books are so magnificent that the words leave whispers in our minds, long after the end of the story. There are those poems or stories that are so astounding that even after you finish them, you put them in your bag, not to read again anytime soon, but just to keep them close to you.'

I heard a titter of laughter, but I also saw a lot of students nodding.

Another student raised her hand tentatively. 'Do you ever struggle to write?'

I gave an exaggerated groan and a ripple of laughter went through the classroom. 'I am struggling right now,' I admitted. 'It is partly why I am here right now. I felt the need to reconnect with people. Kind of like recharging my batteries. But don't spend your energy on complaining that you haven't reached a goal. Spend it on moving forward to make it happen.'

'How?' someone asked.

'Reach for the fruit on the branches, don't wait for gravity to hand it to you. Dreams are only realised when you fight to grab hold of them. Giving the power to fear is taking power from confidence.'

'Wow,' I heard someone breathe.

'Determine the limits of your capabilities and then take one step further. Follow your dreams, even if you have to chase them down. It's far better than waiting for them to come back around. Think about the most basic question:

Why do we tell stories? We do it to distract, to celebrate, to soothe the pain of life.'

'But what if you don't know what to write about?'

'Look around you. Amazing things happen every single day. They can happen with trumpeting fanfare, or silently in a whispered prayer. No one person can keep a running list of these miracles, but they are still there. The difference between a trivial event and a significant one is only that the small one may pass by undetected. Find it. Write about it. You can grasp on to something and hold it tight ... or let it trickle away.'

'You are so successful,' a girl commented, 'but you are in a minority. What about the others who have tried to become writers and failed?'

'The most terrifying things in the world are right inside of you—your power to make either amazing successes or horrible failures,' I responded. 'But it's not enough to want something. You need to earn it first and foremost. And don't look to what other people are doing. When you stand with the crowd, you hide from success.'

I looked around, loving the crackle of inspiration washing over their faces. 'Which leads me to my next subject,' I continued. 'Tell me your stories. Why are you in this class? What brought you to this very moment, sitting in front of me?'

I was exhausted at the end of the class but thrilled at how well everything turned out. The students were attentive and wildly supportive. I hoped that like Arjun inspired me to write, I would be able to extend his gift to my students.

I left them with one last thought: Don't regret anything when your day ends, but use it to inspire greater things the next day.

I didn't have to wait long to learn that I already had. One student approached me when I left the class. 'I can't tell you how amazing it is that you are our professor,' he said, fumbling with his books. 'Your books are an inspiration, and I know that they have changed many people's lives. I have always wanted to be a writer myself but, like you, I didn't know how to start.'

'And now?'

'I'm completely inspired after this class. I can't wait to go back to my dorm, right now, and start writing.'

'Thank you so much for saying that,' I responded. 'I'm sure you're going to have a lot of fun once you get started.'

I bid him goodbye and started walking towards the office. I was planning to head home, but I started to have a thought. It was the smallest hunger, but I recognised that feeling once more. I wanted to write. Not forced, not false.

I was a little apprehensive. Maybe I should let that hunger grow a little bit more? Perhaps I should go home, or drive to see Nisha and Kabir.

No, I decided the urge was strong enough and walked to my office. I was calm and walked at a deliberately slow pace, but my heart was pounding. In my office, I sat down carefully, almost as if I was afraid to dislodge the thought in my mind.

Ah, but it was still there.

First, it was one word that caught my attention and my mind grasped at it. Like an electrical shock, that single word charged through and connected with other words, until they rose up in front of me, each one demanding to be captured by my pen. But in capturing them, I didn't hold them back; I let them fly.

27

FATE

Well, this is an interesting turn of events. Even I have to admit that.

I guess Karma works that way sometimes, though.

I had great plans to destroy these people, to take everything I had given them, and tear it away. I wanted to hurt them, to make them struggle. I wanted them to feel the sense of regret so that it ate them away, destroying their confidence in themselves.

But Vivaan just had to end up in the cab with Parth. I thought I was sending him on a path to rejection, but no, he had to open his mouth and inspire Parth to quit his job and start his own company. And then they ran into each other again? Even I didn't see that coming.

And Kabir. Why did he have to take care of his customers so well? I thought the fire I created would be the end of his happy dreams. But no. He had to run into those students that day. If he had just poured coffee and kept his mouth shut, those students wouldn't have recognised him. He would still be back in his stupid little apartment feeling sorry for himself. Instead, he has been inspired to open a coffee stall.

Then there's Meera. I thought by ruining her book deal, I would have taken away her desire to write. But just look at what has happened! By testing her, by taking away her dream, it inspired her to write an entirely new story!

That's the funny thing about me—fate.

What makes a person great? It's not wishing things will happen, but working to make them happen; they have done that.

People sometimes call me luck. Sometimes luck is good,

and sometimes it is bad. I might be praised or cursed. The handbook of mortality is not about how to die. It's about how to live.

You can bury your head in the sand and ignore a problem, but it doesn't mean it's going to change anything. Just because it's not visible to you doesn't mean it has gone away. Really, it's probably going to be bigger when you do acknowledge it once more. So, don't shut your eyes to your problems—keep them open and face them head-on.

These people learned that. I can challenge, I can test, I can push. Just like I have with these friends. But they changed themselves, and you know what? I can change my colours too.

I think it's time to admit defeat. I tested them, thinking I would break them. But they rose above everything I threw at them.

You can't triumph over someone who refuses to lose.

Perhaps, it is time for their luck to change. It's time for me to change once more.

Have I lost the battle? Never! I'm just changing my mind a little bit about the destruction I've rained down on them. I'm tired of creating chaos. Believe it or not, it is exhausting to keep people on their toes. Even the puppet master grows weary of moving people around.

Everyone has dreams, but not everyone has the courage to follow them. Always move forward and pursue your dreams with ferocious passion.

28

MEERA

'I love you too,' I said into the phone, and hung up, cradling it as I reached to turn off the light.

So much had changed since Vivaan took the job with Parth. At first, he was unsure if he really wanted to move, even though he said it was temporary. When he came home from meeting Parth in Goa, I saw the spark back in his eyes and I knew it was something that I had not been able to give him, no matter how many words I spoke. Parth was able to offer him something tangible, a job.

A job offered him real hope because it gave a reassurance for the future.

In the end, we decided that every minute that passed was one less ahead of us and one more behind us. It was time for Vivaan to embrace his new path.

'I can see something now,' he said, wrapped in my arms the last night before he left Pune. 'I needed to take ownership of my accomplishments as much as my failures.'

'Yes,' I murmured. 'Then put them behind you while holding on to the lesson.'

'Exactly.'

When he left, I charged headfirst into my writing and only came up for air when I spoke with Vivaan on the phone or if I was with Kabir's family. As always, our hopes and dreams were interconnected by threads we couldn't even see or feel. But they were there, keeping our four-sided friendship strong.

I missed Aashi and desperately wanted her back, not just for her amazing organisation skills and all the quiet ways she helped me, but also because her company was soothing. But I couldn't afford to rehire her. I hoped that would change soon, although I didn't know how. Oh well, that was something I would figure out eventually. Let the words come first.

For now, the words were washing over me in waves, and just like one does at the ocean, it didn't really matter if I shifted my feet or took a few steps backward or forward; the waves were still there, faithfully returning after each short retreat.

One day, I stood up and twisted at the waist to release some of the tight muscles. Looking outside, I decided to take a break. It was Tuesday, and I had a suspicion that Kabir might be at the closest coffee stall to my house. At three locations now, it was the newest one, so I had a feeling he would be there to oversee the training.

Sure enough, his smiling face met mine as I approached the newest of the coffee stalls, and a cup of cappuccino was already waiting for me by the time I crossed the street to talk to Kabir.

I took an appreciative sip and moaned. 'This is the perfect way to celebrate a productive day,' I said.

'Another good one, then?' he asked, and I nodded, sipping again. 'Things seem to be on a roll for you these days. Nisha was just saying that you haven't been over in a few days. She misses you but she knows why, and she is so happy that your writing is coming along so well.'

'I'll have to call her on my walk home,' I said, pulling out my purse to pay Kabir. Of course, he argued, but the man would go broke just supporting my coffee habit.

Finally, he grudgingly took my money. 'How is Vivaan doing? Did you speak with him today?'

'Of course,' I said in mock horror that the idea would even cross his mind that I wouldn't speak to Vivaan. 'Every morning and night. And sometimes in between ... although

I have to call him then because he is terrified that he'll be breaking into a thought. Silly boy.'

Kabir nodded. 'I can understand his hesitancy though. Those days that you struggled to write bothered all of us.'

I looked at him, surprised. 'Truly? I know you were all aware that I was frustrated, but I tried to hold it in. We all had so many other things to worry about.'

'Your emotions are like another colour of the rainbow for you,' he said. 'You wear a very distinct colour when you are struggling to write.'

I pursed my lips and thought about his statement for a while. 'Interesting description. Can I use it?' I said with a twinkle in my eye.

He held out his hands in an open gesture. 'What is mine is yours, Meera.'

'You are a good man, Kabir. How is this new stall going?' I asked, watching the other staff taking over to serve other customers.

'Amazing. And just in time. I have another location—'

'What?' I gasped. 'You just got this one up and running!'

He chuckled again and I loved hearing that sound come so naturally to my friend once more. 'I told you, my plan is to have a stall near every college. We are turning such a profit that there is no reason to hold back the expansion.'

'I can think of two reasons to slow down,' I said, half teasing but half serious.

He waved his hand. 'I will never go back to that overworked man again,' he said solemnly. 'Nisha and Jianna come first. Always.'

'Good man,' I said, giving him a pat. 'I better head back now. I think my break is over.'

'Do you want another cappuccino?' he asked. 'One for the road?'

I shook my head. 'I don't want my hands to start shaking

while I'm writing. But I might come back later in the afternoon.' I cocked my eyebrow at him in silent question.

'I won't be here,' he responded. 'We're taking Jianna to the butterfly exhibit again.'

'That sounds even better than coffee,' I sighed. 'But no butterflies for me today. I want to get at least one more chapter written and start polishing up some of the other ones because when I fly to see Vivaan this weekend, I plan to leave my laptop behind.'

'Wow. I'm impressed. Go then!' he said, shooing me away.

I started walking home, thinking about all the changes we had gone through since the day I ran into Arjun at the Delhi Lit Fest. It seemed so long ago; we had all lived a lifetime with the challenges that had been thrown at us since then.

No matter who you are, or what you have done, there is a moment that you want to give in to failure.

But that wasn't right, was it? If time just went on and on, with no ending and no beginning, how could we treasure each day?

I never imagined it would be so tough, but success comes with a price tag. Sometimes you have to do much more than you expected to taste the sweet moment of success.

Accept fate, but determine to make some changes in your life. By doing this, you learn more about yourself and it gives you the incentive to pursue your dreams. You might need to return to the starting line, but use it as an opportunity to run the race in a different way.

Our stories were far from over and as I turned the lock and pushed the front door to my house open, I was buoyed by this effervescent hope.

Resolve to look at your life's challenges in the eye. Persist and move forward. I was ready to do that.

29

VIVAAN

One year later

Isn't fate a funny, fickle thing? One minute I was on top of the world. The next moment, I was thrown further down than I had ever been. My dreams were shattered, and I was lower, more depressed than I had ever been, even when working as a banker.

Then things started to look up once more. The end is not the final moment, but a bridge to the next beginning. We don't realise it until we take that next step. No matter what you may learn, one of the most valuable lessons you can learn is that of patience. Sometimes it takes a long time to work through something that should take a much shorter time.

In a storm, surrounded by rain and wind and despair, it is hard to even remember the sun will shine again. I even forgot the feel of the warmth on my face for a little while. But the storm did pass and I emerged a changed man.

When those first rays of sun hit my face again, I appreciated them all the more. I embraced the lessons of the storm, but cherished the relief as it passed. Life's experiences can be wonderful or harsh, but the harsh lessons are meant to help, not hurt.

I was pleasantly surprised to realise how much I enjoyed working with Parth and his company. Gone was that depressed man I got to know in the Uber. Instead, he threw all his energy into making Yaadein a thriving success. He split his marketing efforts between seniors and their family members, travelling across India to give talks about the importance of capturing this precious history. It complemented the rich history our country has. Knowing how much I love travelling, Parth made sure that I had the opportunity to travel with him sometimes as well. Managing the financial aspects was critical—even more, as the company skyrocketed—but I found myself caught up in the excitement of this prospering business so much that every day I worked at Yaadein was invigorating.

'It's amazing how fast Yaadein continues to grow,' I mused, walking hand in hand with Meera. Despite our busy schedules, she and I made sure to take time out for us, too. Today, we were visiting the Pune Okayama Friendship Garden and were enjoying a brisk walk on a rare cold day. 'It seems like every time I open my laptop, I find another retirement community or nursing home that wants to contract with us.'

Meera shivered a little and pulled her jacket around her shoulders tightly. 'It sounds like Parth is going to have to bring on more writers,' she said. 'Let me know if he wants me to speak with some of my students again.' In a brilliant move several months ago, Parth and Meera combined forces to give some of her students the opportunity to hone their writing skills by working for Yaadein on a part-time basis.

'I definitely will,' I responded, wrapping my arm around her and rubbing her arms briskly to warm her up. 'Do you want to head back to the car?'

She shook her head. 'The chill in the air is actually a nice relief after all the heat we've had lately. Besides, I love this place. The Japanese influences are such an interesting change from the other gardens in Pune.'

We stopped and took in the well-manicured lawns and the trees that, to me, were cut to look like children's lollipops. I couldn't help but laugh every time I saw the happy-looking branches.

A gust of wind rose and blew, pushing us along the path toward the waterfalls.

'How is your blog doing, by the way?' she asked.

'Talk about taking off,' I said happily. 'It astounds me how much people are enjoying my pictures and my writing. Now I completely understand how much you love to write; it's humbling but amazing to get so much attention and such positive feedback from people across the world!'

'How wonderful.'

I thought about the huge milestone that took place last week when my Instagram posts reached one million followers. Meera was obviously reading my mind because she mused, 'A million people… it's absolutely amazing. And how about the sponsorships?'

'I'm still trying to figure out which ones I really want to promote,' I said. 'You know how much I love Puma, but then Nike and Adidas are fantastic companies as well. Oh, I didn't tell you, I did sign with UCB the other day.'

'Ooo,' she responded. 'I could go for a nice layer of that right now!'

We laughed, thoroughly delighting in each other's company before my next trip. It seemed like every time I turned around, someone wanted to fly me to another part of India to check out a hotel or resort. Tomorrow, I was heading to Chennai to check out a new hotel on the beach. I was hoping that Meera would be able to come with me, but with final terms coming up, she felt it was important to stay behind to help some of her struggling students.

She was so dedicated towards her students and took the time to help those who might be finding the class particularly challenging. 'How is Siddharth doing, by the way?' She loved to tell me stories about this particular young man. Although he was dyslexic, he had such a passion for reading and writing that Meera pitched in quite often to help him when he was having difficulties.

Meera smiled happily. 'I paired him up with another student, who is helping him by reading his work out loud to him. I do believe they might be developing into more than just two study partners.'

'You little matchmaker,' I teased.

'I honestly wouldn't have thought the two of them would be a good match,' she said. 'Well, at least, not until she jumped at the chance to help him. Then I realised there might have been a bit of a crush there.'

'And Siddharth?'

'Oh, there is definitely some interest. He shows up for class early each time now, and he even got a haircut!'

'No!'

Meera nodded. 'He's totally cleaned up now. And I'm pretty sure it's all because of his study partner. They arrive separately, but they sit together and leave side by side now.'

My phone pinged and I realised that we would have to head home soon. 'I think we're going to have to cut this short,' I said regretfully. 'Let's head back to the car and you can tell me the latest in your writing.'

'No way,' she said. 'I want to hear more about the trip we're going on next month when the semester is out.'

'I think you're going to love it,' I said. 'I'll have to show you pictures later. The resort has these little separate huts with huge, thatched roofs. It looks like the huts are actually part of the jungle with all the old growth they were able to preserve. I can't imagine how that big construction equipment managed to do it, but they did.'

'And there's a pool?' she asked again. Meera did love spending time by the pool. Of course, since she brought her journal everywhere she went, she certainly could write anywhere.

'There are either two or three pools; I can't remember.'

'What about the food?' she pressed.

'Well, since we're part of the pilot programme being brought in to test the accommodations, we'll have to see how good the dining is. But it sounds like they are bringing in several chefs from different culinary specialties and we get to pick which foods we like the best.'

Meera clapped happily. For such a petite woman, she certainly could pack away the food. 'Oh, I can't wait,' she said excitedly.

We reached the car but before we drove away, I used my phone to check my email again. 'Hey, guess what!' I said excitedly.

'What?'

'It looks like I might be heading back to Goa again soon. There is a new hotel they want me to blog about,' I said, scrolling through the email. 'And, they asked if we might have some friends who want to come along, preferably with kids. It looks like they need to test a couple of different demographics.'

'Oh, fun! Do you think Nisha and Kabir will be able to get away?'

I nodded. 'I know they're busy, but I bet they'll make time for this. Jianna will love it!'

I turned my phone off and leaned over the seat to kiss Meera, long and passionately. When we caught our breath again, Meera grinned at me. 'What was that all about?' she giggled.

I shook my head. 'I'm just so amazingly happy. I would never have thought a year ago, when things were so bad, that we would be here right now, planning these trips together. It's amazing how our luck has turned.'

'Hope is real. It's good. And good never goes away. And it's our hard work,' she laughed. 'We are good people and we deserve happiness. Plus, we never gave up, not in each other and not in ourselves.'

30

KABIR

'You're back again?' I laughed at my new friend and started making his favourite double espresso. 'Finals week is pretty tough, huh?'

My customer propped his elbow up on the counter and sighed heavily, then took a deep whiff as the aroma of the coffee reached his nose. 'Mm...' he groaned appreciatively. 'I have no idea how I would have gotten through my exams without your coffee.'

I grinned and said, 'Probably the same way you did last year before I set up shop here.'

At that, the young man shuddered in remembrance. 'Yeah, and I blew two of my exams last year because I kept falling asleep while I was studying!'

I handed him his travel cup and took his money. 'Well, as many of those as you've pounded back in the last few days, you probably won't go to sleep until the next semester starts!'

My young friend gave me a winning smile and said, 'That's the plan, definitely.' As he took his change, I realised his hand was shaking ever so slightly. At first, I dismissed it as caffeine jitters but just as he was about to turn away, I thought about the lunch that Nisha had packed for me. I knew she had packed extra jeera biscuits, knowing that they were my favourite. 'Hey,' I said and he turned back to me. 'You are eating, right?' I couldn't help but worry about some of these kids; they pushed themselves so hard at the end of the term.

'Yeah, this morning,' he said confidently before his smile started to fade.

'Wait. Hm.'

I didn't give him a chance to say anything else. I lifted up my cooler and started to reach in for some of the biscuits. Seeing the hungry look in his eye, I wrapped a few biscuits in a napkin and then pulled out one of the two Russian Salad sandwiches that Nisha had packed. 'Here,' I said, putting the food into a small paper bag and handing it to him. 'My wife makes the best sandwiches.'

'Really?' he said, incredulously. 'Wow, thank you!'

I smiled happily. 'Well, when your exams are done, and you don't need quite so much coffee, I expect you to come back and let me know how well you did!'

He was already munching on Nisha's biscuit. 'I will,' he said around a mouthful of food. 'This is delicious,' he said, reminding me of Jianna with cookie crumbs on his face.

'I'll tell my wife,' I offered. 'She'll be very happy to hear it. Wait until you try the sandwich. You can't get any better in a restaurant.'

'I can't wait,' he said happily. 'You are one lucky man, Kabir!'

I nodded. 'I know it,' I responded before I gave him a wave to send him back to his dorm room. 'Don't I know it,' I said more quietly to myself.

And I did know how fortunate I was. The coffee stall near Pune University was so successful that we were turning a profit in no time. I wasn't able to run it by myself, so I hired a staff member to help. And as soon as I was able to, I hired several more staff to help with the long shifts.

With the profits, Nisha and I agreed that we would invest in another coffee stall near one of the other universities in Pune. Word caught on quickly and we were extremely busy there as well.

In the next few months, we expanded so that ten campuses had a Kabir coffee stall near it. I carefully and personally trained each staff member until I was convinced that they understood every coffee recipe I had created, but also the nuances of running a coffee booth.

Yet, all this time, I kept the memory of my horrible burns fresh in my mind, and the promise I made to myself when I was healing to always put my family first. So, no matter how busy I was, and no matter how busy Nisha was with our little girl, we always took time for ourselves, whether it was sharing a cuddle in the early morning before we got up, or going out to eat. Often, we took Jianna but sometimes, we hired a babysitter to watch her so we could have some 'us' time.

I was working as hard as I did when Kafe Kabir was open, but now that I took the time with my family, my time at work was much more pleasurable. I no longer felt torn, trying to figure out what was more important: making money to support my family or being with my family.

How much I would have missed watching Jianna growing up had fate not stepped in that day, and caused that devastating fire. At the time, and while we were struggling to make ends meet, I would stay up long into the night, cursing fate for its cruelty. I now realised that if it wasn't for that disastrous day, I would never have stopped.

I knew we needed to work on us every single day. We needed to work to support each other's hopes and dreams and to share happiness and sadness. It wasn't always going to be the easiest thing in the world in many ways, but in others, it would be so simple, because it was a part of us.

At first, when I mentioned the fact that I was thankful for the accident to Nisha, I'm pretty sure she thought I was finally going crazy, judging by the funny look on her face. It happened to be one day when we were walking through my favourite path, the one on the university with the old trees that were pushing their way on to the walkway. It was one of Jianna's favourites, too. She loved pretending she was a princess in a magical garden.

'I mean it,' I said to Nisha's doubting face. 'What would have happened to us if Kafe Kabir was still there? I don't know if I would have ever realised how important it was to make time for you two.'

Ever the supportive wife, I could tell Nisha was getting ready to defend my own actions to me. I held up a hand to stop her. 'I know what you're going to say but honestly, at what point do you think I would have slowed down?

She stopped and considered my question, slowly shaking her head. 'I don't know if you would have,' she finally admitted. 'But I don't know about actually being happy that you were hurt. That was horrible. I almost lost you, Kabir.'

Nisha bumped into me on the walkway, and I knew she needed a hug. I stopped walking and took her into my arms. 'But you didn't lose me,' I said sincerely and gently kissed the frown lines on her forehead. With one eye on Jianna, we stood like that for several minutes, just rocking gently under the towering old trees. 'And now, you have more of me that I didn't really know was in me to give.'

Jianna came galloping back to us, and I bent down so she could launch herself into my arms. 'Group hug!' she yelled happily, throwing her chubby arms around us.

We started walking again, turning our attention back to talking about the coffee stands and filling each other on bits of conversations we had with Vivaan and Meera. Finally, I broached a subject that had been on my mind since the day Kafe Kabir burned down, but I pushed away until the success of the coffee stalls made it a real possibility.

'Nisha,' I said hesitantly. 'We are doing really well with our coffee stalls now. And we can hardly keep up, now that the end-of-term finals are on.'

'Yes, I know,' she said. In fact, while I was busy running

the businesses, she was the one who was tracking the finances. The day the average monthly profits from each stall broke the thirty-thousand rupee , she surprised me with a delicious home-cooked meal, going all out and cooking all day. And then one day, I came home to find her all dressed up with reservations to an upscale restaurant across town. I thought she was just surprising me with a nice meal, only to find out later that it was to honour the coffee booths each making more than fifty thousand rupees each month.

She definitely had an even better sense of our finances than I did.

'What would you think if we rebuilt?'

She stopped again on the path so abruptly that a student walking behind us almost ran into her. I tugged her to one side, apologising to the student. The student waved off the apology. 'Love your coffee,' she said and passed us with a grin.

When we were alone again, I repeated my question. 'Rebuild Kafe Kabir?' she asked, her eyes wide.

I nodded. 'I don't think we would need to take out a large loan at all, and now we have all ten coffee booths to use as collateral so we should get a really good interest rate.'

Her eyes flashed and I knew she was thinking about the fire again. 'That isn't going to happen again, Nisha,' I whispered.

'How do you know?' Her eyes filled with tears. 'We never thought it would happen the first time!'

I took a deep breath. 'We'll hire the best electricians and make sure the wiring is absolutely perfect,' I said. 'And we won't use old, used equipment that we need to keep patching. Everything will be brand new.'

'And safe?'

'And safe. I promise, Nisha. I can fail and I can break. But in breaking, I can still find a way to piece my dreams back together. Each morning heralds a new day and today is the day I think I should start rebuilding.'

'I know this is something you have wanted,' she said slowly. 'I always knew you wanted to rebuild, but I don't think I realised that I was scared of the idea until now when it looks like it could become a reality again.'

I reached out to put my arm around her. 'I didn't realise it was at the back of your mind,' I responded gently. 'I can't imagine what you must have gone through when I was injured.'

She nodded. 'What you say makes sense, Kabir. I know we will be more careful this time. There is something else to think about. The timing.'

My brow furrowed in question. 'I don't think the timing could be better. We are turning a very good, steady profit now.'

'I know that we are,' she said. 'But don't forget that the semester will be ending next week. That booming business you have … it is probably going to fall off quite a bit.'

I thought about it. 'That is a valid point,' I said. 'But one of the reasons we chose these specific locations is because they are near the largest schools and colleges in Pune. Yes, I'm sure business will fall off a little bit since this is the last semester, but don't forget campuses use that time for conferences and other events. I really don't think we're going to see as much of a drop in business as we did.'

'That is true,' Nisha mused. 'On the other hand, with this being the lightest time of year for educational institutions, this is probably the best time to plan and build, right?'

I loved the way this woman thought. Of the two of us, she was the more cautious one, but it only meant that she thought things over when I might tend to leap first and ask questions later. We truly balanced each other perfectly. 'I didn't even think of that,' I admitted.

She nudged me. 'Well, this is why you keep me around, right?'

'One of the many reasons,' I said sincerely. 'Let's go home and start thinking about where we want to locate the new and improved Kafe Kabir.'

31

MEERA

The end.

I typed out those six letters and sat back in my chair. That was it, the story was complete. Of course, there would be edits, and some areas would still need to be fleshed out. But my new manuscript, once it started, practically wrote itself. I was only wielding the instrument as it took on a life of its own.

I was aware of a dull ache in my neck. How long had I been sitting there? I reached over for my cup of cappuccino, only to realise it was cold... and completely untouched. I smiled to myself. As this book was being written, countless cups of cappuccino suffered from my inattention. I craned my neck and rubbed at the ache, trying to tease the knot out of the muscle while it was just a nuisance and not a full-blown stiff neck.

A bath would help, I decided. To be honest, I couldn't remember if I had taken a shower that morning, and I definitely couldn't remember the last time I had soaked in a nice hot bath. It was time to take care of this body a little bit.

Before I slipped into the bath though, I called Vivaan.

'Hey,' he said when he answered the phone. 'You are emerging from your cave at last?'

I laughed and took in a deep, cleansing breath. 'It's done.'

'Wait a minute.' I heard a shuffling on the other end and I pictured him sitting up a little straighter, holding the phone in his hand instead of cradling it under his shoulder while he half talked, half worked. 'It's done?' he repeated.

'Mmm,' I said happily. 'I'm going to go take a bath to celebrate. I have a horrible stiff neck.'

'I'm surprised you don't have a completely stiff body,' he said dryly. 'You hardly moved from that chair for the last week and a half.'

'I was on a roll,' I said. 'I do believe you know what that's like now, Mr Blog Extraordinaire.' Considering our vastly different backgrounds, I truly enjoyed that we had some common ground that we could talk over with each other. Now that he knew how much time and effort went into writing a thousand-word blog, he truly appreciated the time and energy it took to write a book.

'Yes, I do,' he said. 'But tell me more … it's really done?'

'Except for the edits,' I clarified, and he groaned sympathetically.

'When do I get to read it? Tell me you're not going to make me wait through the editing process!'

'Actually,' I said, 'I'd really like it if you could read it now.'

'I'll be right over.'

I loved the man's enthusiasm. 'Slow down,' I urged. 'Let a girl get a bath first. Can you come over tonight?'

'Absolutely. How about I bring dinner?'

'That would be perfect. I'll see you in a couple of hours.'

I left the office and walked back to the kitchen where Aashi was happily looking over some of my writing. She looked up at me and smiled. I gave her a big grin and nodded, confirming that it was done.

'I think you should take the rest of the afternoon off,' I said.

'Oh, I don't mind working a little more,' she said. Ever since she had returned, she was even more dedicated about helping me.

I hugged her and sang out, 'Vivaan's coming over.'

'Oh! And you want a little alone time.'

I laughed out, delighted once more at the sound coming from my throat. It felt so good to laugh.

A few minutes later, I stepped into my hot bath, thinking about the manuscript I had just finished. When I started working in my teaching position, the students' curiosity about the genesis of my first book, 'Everyone Has a Story', made my thoughts turn to everything that had happened to the main characters in that book—the four of us—when life started challenging us in unexpected ways.

We all faced different crises, but just as our lives were intertwined, our reliance on each other brought us closer together as we struggled to overcome those challenges.

You can get lost on the journey to your goals, but along the way, you find something more important. You find out who you truly are.

As inspirational as my readers found the first book, and as curious as they were about the characters, I decided that the perfect next step for me would be to write the sequel, detailing our challenges and how fate threatened to destroy our happiness.

And how we all persevered, through laughter and tears... a lot of tears... Well, and a lot of laughter too.

I watched Nisha and Kabir struggling after the fire but also witnessed the two grow closer together than ever before. Now, with ten coffee stands and rebuilding Kafe Kabir, as well as a rambunctious three-year-old, it would stand to reason that they would be too busy for each other. Instead, they continued to carve out time for themselves.

It was an honour to bear witness to their success, and an even greater honour to be able to write their continued story.

Then there was Vivaan and me. I thought back to that horrible day when the drug charges were filed against him. Months and months later, Shridhar, Vivaan's seatmate, was caught with drugs again. Parth heard about it, remembered the name, and had his company's lawyer take a statement from Shridhar, exonerating Vivaan from any wrongdoing. By then, Vivaan was already rebuilding his name and reputation, but having that piece of paper seemed to help settle that unease that Vivaan felt was plaguing him all those horrible months.

And I was able to detail that piece of information in my book when I wove in our part into the manuscript.

The sequel, I decided as I lay in the steaming water, surrounded by decadent bubbles, was the perfect example of staying true to ourselves and keeping an eye on our dreams. Although there were many times when we might have doubted we would get a second chance at those hopes and wishes, we never doubted our abilities.

I was dressed in a cotton summer dress when Vivaan came over, his arms overflowing with Chinese food. The moment we devoured our meal, Vivaan carefully washed his hands and then eagerly asked to look at the manuscript.

'I printed you a copy, in case you wanted to take it home tonight,' I said bashfully. Even after all this time, I still had my shy moments about my writing.

He gave me a huge smile, tugged the printed copy out of my hand and sat down to read. I wandered into the kitchen and poured myself a glass of water while I cleaned up the kitchen. When I returned to the living room twenty minutes later, he barely looked up.

I sat down and pulled out the book I had been reading before I maniacally started writing the last couple weeks. Every now and then, I would look up, but he kept his eyes on the words in front of him.

Finally, I started yawning and realised I had gotten up at three-thirty that morning to write. 'I think I'm going to go to bed,' I said regretfully. 'Are you going to head home?'

He looked up. 'If you don't mind, I think I'm going to sit here for a while longer.'

I sat down beside him. 'Do you like it?' I asked eagerly.

With huge eyes, he nodded soberly. 'It's amazing,' he said. I went to kiss him again but a yawn escaped my lips. 'Go to bed,' he ordered. 'I'll lock the door behind me when I leave.'

'Okay,' I agreed and half walked, half staggered to the bedroom.

The room was completely dark when I heard my bedroom door open. 'Vivaan?' I asked sleepily.

'Yeah,' he responded softly.

'What time is it?'

He laughed lowly. 'It's about four in the morning.'

Wide awake now, I sat up in bed. 'You're still here?'

The mattress sagged as he sat beside me. 'I couldn't stop reading your book. It was ... amazing. How you captured all those emotions of what happened to us. I'm in awe of you,' he said and wrapped his arms around me.

We talked for a while and fell asleep together. When I woke up a couple hours later, I opened my eyes to take in his grinning face.

'I can't wait to get your book out there,' he said eagerly.

I sighed. 'One problem. I still don't have a publisher.'

'I've been thinking about it,' Vivaan said. 'Let's go make some coffee and I'll explain.'

Together we wandered into the kitchen. 'Sit,' he ordered and began bustling around to make coffee for us. It wasn't Kafe Kabir coffee, but our friend had shown us enough tricks of the trade so we could both manage a half decent cup.

'So tell me what you're thinking,' I prompted.

'Well,' he began, 'remember when I told you someone asked me if I could put my blog articles into a full book form and publish it myself?'

'Yes.'

'I started to look into it a bit. I'm still not sure that's the best solution for me, but, Meera, I think it's a good idea for you.'

'Me? Self-publish?' I asked incredulously. 'It never really occurred to me before.'

'I think it's a fantastic idea. I mean, look at your fan base. Just your students alone have you on this pedestal—a well-deserved one, I might add—and they are only a select group. You have so many followers ... they don't care where the next book comes from, they just want to read it!'

I thought about it through several sips of my coffee. 'That just might work,' I said.

'I think it would.' He threw his arms wide in emphasis. 'I know it will! Do you remember Pari telling us during our last trip to Goa that she had a friend who was an artist? That woman had created a bunch of book covers... we could contact her, and I bet she would have some ideas of who else we could go to help us get this self-published.'

I looked at him, simultaneously touched and amazed by his excitement. 'You are an incredibly wonderful man, you know it?'

He stood up and pulled me into a tight embrace. 'I am everything I can be to make you love me,' he said. 'The person I am, Meera, is because of you. Because of your love, because of your support. When I think about how easily you could have turned your back on me last year when I was accused of possessing drugs...'

'No,' I said quickly. 'I would never, ever turn my back on you Vivaan. You are the other part of my soul. Everybody is challenged at some point in their life and we were no different. We learned a very valuable lesson through all that. When we turned to each other instead of turning inward to nurse our own hurt hearts, we gave each other the strength we needed.'

With Vivaan's idea, I knew my book was going to come to fruition even quicker than we could even imagine. It was amazing to think that when fate intervened, how rapidly life could change. And this time, it was definitely for the better.

EPILOGUE

FATE

You didn't expect to see me again, did you?

I know, I know. You didn't like me for a long time … but come on, life gets boring. People take advantage of the good times and they really don't stop to appreciate them like they should.

I just … spice things up a little bit.

Vivaan finished training his replacement and left Yaadein, but kept his stock options. Parth was very grateful that he stayed as long as he did to make sure the transition went smoothly, but his replacement is quite a capable young woman. I think she'd make a great partner for him in many ways...

As Vivaan's popularity grew, he had to hire a digital marketing assistant, kind of a male version of Aashi, but with more technical prowess. Vivaan was more than happy to have an assistant so he could be on hand while Meera was doing her book tours. As he predicted, her book was widely successful, topping the bestseller list in a matter of days. And those publishers that turned their backs on her before? Now they're lining up to capture her attention.

Not only are there publishers calling her all the time, but Bollywood has been knocking on her door, too, so to speak. With Vivaan by her side, she has spoken to a few of them but hasn't made any decision yet on the movie rights.

Speaking of spicing things up, I got a front-row seat when Kafe Kabir was reopened. Of course, Meera and Vivaan were there with Kabir and Nisha while they celebrated the grand opening of the café. I really thought they did a very tasteful job of pulling in some of the elements from the old café, like the comfortable white leather seats in the corner while making this one different at the same time.

You'll be happy to know that I nudged one of the best electricians in the city towards one of Kabir's coffee stalls. After meeting Kabir, he cleared his calendar to make sure he could do the electrical work on the new building.

You can't see me, but I'm in the chair right across from Meera and Vivaan.

Waiting.

For what, you may ask. What could possibly keep fate waiting?

A few things, really. I do have a tendency to nudge things along.

But there are a few times in a person's life when I do like to sit back and wait for things to happen on their own. It must be the romantic in me.

'I'm tired of fighting,' Meera starts with a little sigh.

Oh, I know where this is going. This is going to be good.

Vivaan looks at her like she has just sprouted another head. 'Fighting? We're not fighting!'

'Yes,' she responds. 'You and I have been fighting a battle of sorts for many years. First, we struggled to get to know each other, even though we were haunted by the past. Then, you and I did battle, not with each other, but with the things that held us back from realizing our dreams. You had to leave your position as a banker to finally make your dream come true to travel. And I needed to fight my insecurities and gain confidence in my writing.'

'That is true.'

'Then, there was the terrible year last year when everything seemed to be coming together for us but fate...' She spits out my name bitterly. *Ouch*. 'Fate decided to mess things up for us and pushed our dreams off track.'

'But we kept fighting,' Vivaan says.

'We did. Our strength was that we knew our love and our dreams were worth fighting for.'

She reaches out to hold Vivaan's hands. 'They were that day and they still are now.' Vivaan starts to say something but Meera shushes him. 'One special thing happened last year, though. It happened right before things went crazy in our lives.'

'Which was?'

'You took me to that amazing restaurant and then you asked me to think about the possibility of marrying you.'

He nods softly and a smile begins to bloom on his face. 'I remember.'

'I didn't handle it very well then,' she admits. 'But I'm ready to bring up the subject again.'

'You're ready to talk about marriage?' Vivaan asks happily.

'No,' she says.

'No?'

'No.' And with that, she drops to her knee and the words rush out of her. 'I'm not ready to talk about it. I'm ready to do it. Vivaan.' She stops and kisses his hand. 'Will you do me the honour of becoming my husband? We love each other, and we bring our own complexities to the table. That isn't going to make for a boring life together, but a unique, adventurous one.'

By then, everyone in the café has turned to them. I can hear the soft clicks of cell phone cameras being snapped.

Meera looks up at him expectantly before he bursts out with a 'YES!' that echoes through the stones around them. Meera jumps to her feet, throws her arms around him, and the two start laughing and crying at the same time.

'Why here?' Vivaan asks, tears of happiness beginning to gather in the corner of his eyes.

'At Kafe Kabir? Because it's where everything started for us. It might not be the same place, but in a way, it is, with our friends around us.'

Right on cue, Kabir and Nisha make their way over and the four exchange hugs. Then, Meera falls into his arms once more, laughing before they share another long kiss. And then another.

Between kisses, Meera pulls back with a mock serious look on her face. 'I don't have a ring for you, though.'

And with that, Vivaan pulls out his wallet where he has a gorgeous engagement ring stashed. 'I do,' he says happily and slips it on to her finger before the couple embraces once more to happy applause.

Through happy tears, Meera exclaims, 'When did you get that ring?'

He smiles and looks right in my direction. Well yes, maybe I did drop the suggestion to him. Yep. Call me a romantic.

On the other hand, those two deserved fate smiling down on them. After all, they took everything I could manage to throw at them and still managed to rein me in. That's okay, I don't mind admitting defeat. At times like this, I am more than happy to sit back and watch them enjoy the rewards they earned by defeating me.

Is this happily ever after? Only time will tell.

But for now, I am done with them. It is time to turn my attention elsewhere.

I have a new job, a new path to shake up.

I am coming to test you next. Yes YOU, my reader. I am coming to destroy you.

Will you pass my tests, or fail? Only time will tell.

Are you ready? Or are you scared?

THANK YOU

To My Readers,

Thank you for joining me in telling the new chapters of the lives of Meera, Vivaan, Kabir & Nisha. I hope they touched your soul the same way they touched mine.

To the ones who write encouraging emails or speak to me in person on the road ... your feedback means the world to me. Thank you!

To the ones who pass on books they've enjoyed to friends, relatives, and neighbours, you are multiplying the impact of each book. Thank you!

To the ones who write passionately negative reviews ... your feedback challenges me to write more effectively in the future. Thank you!

Thank you for interacting with me, sharing your lives with me, and being the reason I can continue doing what I love.

If you loved this book and have a minute to spare, I would really appreciate a short review on the page or site where you bought the book. Your help in spreading the word is greatly appreciated.

You're all amazing!

With profound gratitude,
Savi

ACKNOWLEDGEMENTS

First and above all, I praise the Universe for guiding me towards the purpose of my life.

My family and friends for their love, support and trust on me.

Special thanks to Deepthi Talwar, my sweet editor, for saving me the embarrassment of making terrible mistakes. Thank you, Neha Khanna for not just being an amazing author relationship manager but a beautiful soul sister.

I am grateful to the entire team at Westland Ltd., led by Gautam Padmanabhan, for their untiring efforts in helping my stories reach you.

Thank you, Ashish Bagrecha, without your efforts and encouragements, I could not become the storyteller I am today, and I understand how difficult it was for you, therefore, I can just say thanks for everything and hope the Universe gives you all the best in return. Your poetries and writings heal people and hope you publish your book soon.

AUTHOR BIO

Savi Sharma, 25, is a simple girl from Surat who left her CA studies to become a storyteller. She self-published her inspirational novel, *Everyone Has a Story* which was acquired later by Westland Publications.

More than 250,000 copies of her debut novel has been since its release in June 2016 and is India's fastest selling debut novel.

Her second novel, *This Is Not Your Story* released in February 2017 and became an instant bestseller with over 150,000 copies been sold and received rave reviews.

Her books and her success story have inspired millions of people in following their dreams, fighting failures, believing in love and writing their own stories of life.

Everyone Has a Story – 2 is her third novel and a sequel to her widely successful debut novel.

You can connect with her on www.savisharma.com or follow @storytellersavi on Facebook, Twitter & Instagram.